December's Secrets

Secrets

A Larry Macklin Mystery-Book 2

A. E. Howe

Books in the Larry Macklin Mystery Series:

November's Past (Book 1)

December's Secrets (Book 2)

January's Betrayal (Book 3)

February's Regrets (Book 4)

March's Luck (Book 5)

April's Desires (Book 6)

Copyright © 2016 A. E Howe

ISBN: 0-9862733-7-6
ISBN-13: 978-0-9862733-7-7

DEDICATION

For Melanie—my friend, my partner, my muse and my wife. Thanks for making every part of my life better.

CHAPTER ONE

The winds of December were bringing in frigid air. High humidity and low temperatures can deliver bone-chilling cold, even in north Florida. Shivering a bit, I watched the crime scene techs try to cut the corpse from the tree without damaging any evidence that might have been on the rope it hung from.

Uncharitably, I was glad that the man was white. I really didn't want to deal with all the racial connotations that would come if the victim had been black. The corpse was wearing cargo pants, cheap hiking boots and a plaid shirt over a long-sleeve undershirt. From what I could see from the ground, he looked to be in his mid-thirties. His hair was brown and uncut. His swollen facial features made it hard to tell much more about him. The body had been discovered earlier this morning after dispatch received an anonymous tip.

Shantel Williams and Marcus Brown, two of our Adams County crime techs, were being assisted by three more from the Florida Department of Law Enforcement. Since we're a small county of less than thirty thousand, we often call on FDLE to assist us with major crimes. Having Tallahassee in the next county over had its advantages.

They had rigged up a second rope so they could cut the rope used for the hanging, but still be able to lower the body gently to the ground. A van from the coroner's office was waiting to take it to the morgue in Tallahassee.

"Be careful now. No need breaking any bones that aren't already broken," Shantel told the guys who were lowering the body. The mocha-skinned middle-aged woman took charge of any situation she found herself in. And when things went wrong, even when it was no fault of her own, she was the first one to take the blame.

A few minutes after the body was placed on the ground, she came over to me holding the dead man's wallet open in her gloved hand so that I could read the information on his driver's license. "At least you won't have to waste time trying to figure out who he is," she said.

"Very considerate of him to keep his wallet with him during his brutal execution," I told her.

"Don't be a smartass. It's too cold for that. You know I'm supposed to be Christmas shopping this morning? I had the day off. Esther and I had the whole day planned... Going to go to Tallahassee and shop until we dropped. But you all just had to find a dead body. Out in these woods, it could have hung here for another day without someone finding it," Shantel said, shaking her head. "You think Marcus is going to be happy? Esther is *not* going to be in a good mood."

Marcus and Shantel worked together almost every day and Marcus's wife, Esther, was Shantel's best friend. Hey, it was a small town and an even smaller sheriff's department. Though I knew she didn't want to hear it now, I was glad they had called her in. Marcus and Shantel were the best crime scene techs in the department.

While Shantel ranted on about having to come in to work, I wrote down the man's name and vitals: 5'10", 200 pounds, brown eyes, brown hair. Doug Timberlane. The name didn't ring any bells with me.

Looking over at our unmarked car, I could see my

partner, Pete Henley, texting furiously on his phone. Considering the size of the big man's chubby fingers, he always impressed me with his dexterity. "Pete!" I yelled. He continued texting. "Pete, put your damn phone away and come over here."

He typed for another second, apparently hit "send" and looked up. "You don't have teenage daughters." He brought his three-hundred-plus pounds to an upright position and came lumbering over to me.

"Ever hear of a Doug Timberlane?" I asked.

"That him?" He pointed to the body.

"No, I'm pulling random names out of my ass to ask you about."

"He's in one of his smartass moods," Shantel said while she bagged and tagged the wallet.

"No. There are some Timberlys that live north of town, but I can't say I know any Timberlanes," Pete said. I made fun of him, but Pete had an encyclopedic knowledge of the people and the history of Adams County. I had seen him solve more than one case simply by making connections between people, their families and their friends.

"According to his wallet, he lives on Sawgrass Road in the north end of the county," I told him.

"There are quite a few trailers and old houses for rent out that way."

I knew the area because of frequent calls for service when I was on the road. There were plenty of domestic abuse and overdose calls and all the other crimes that went with unemployment, poverty and substance abuse.

"If you'll keep an eye on things here I'll ride up there. Maybe I can find some family or friends," I said to Pete, who was checking his phone again. "Only if you can tear yourself away from your messages."

"Yeah, yeah. Go, I got this," Pete said good-naturedly.

I turned the heat up as I drove out on the dirt road that led back to the main highway. The murder site appeared more secluded than it actually was. Go a hundred yards any direction, you'd run into a neighborhood. We were just south of Calhoun, the county seat. I knew a woman who lived not too far away. We had dated a couple times and I still had hopes that it might become a real relationship. Unfortunately, she wasn't comfortable getting involved with a sheriff's deputy.

I thought about driving by Cara's duplex, but decided that would be too stalkerish. I headed on into town, going through a dozen or so stoplights and passing the large courthouse in the square. The car bounced over the railroad tracks that still divided Calhoun into the haves and the have-nots. I drove past the warehouse parking lot where a murder had recently taken place. I'd gotten lucky solving the case. I'd gotten lucky *surviving* the case.

Fifteen minutes later I turned onto Sawgrass Road and began checking numbers on houses and mailboxes. It was a challenge in this rundown area. Many of the numbers were missing or impossible to read. When I finally found Timberlane's address, I was looking at a mobile home that was at least twenty years old, faded and neglected. Pulling up in the driveway, it was obvious that this guy was not a high roller. The grass in the yard hadn't been cut for months and was brown and dry from the recent frosts.

There was an old pickup in the driveway. When I called in the tag, it came back registered to a David Tyler. We hadn't found any vehicles close to the site of the hanging, so I didn't know if Timberlane had a car or not. This could have certainly been his truck—he wouldn't be the first poor guy who didn't have the money to get all the paperwork right on his vehicle. I looked in the windows and saw the front seat was covered in fast food bags and cups, discarded cigarette packs and other trash. Nothing unusual or helpful—no bloodstains or the other half of the rope he was hung with.

I climbed the trailer's rickety wooden stairs and knocked

on the door. No answer. I walked around to the back door. No luck there either. But I spotted an old man sitting on the screened porch of the equally dilapidated home next door. I waved and he took a hand out from underneath a pile of blankets to wave back.

"Kind of cold to be sitting outside," I shouted to him.

"Fresh air. Gotta have my air," he answered in a voice gravelly from too much smoking and drinking.

I walked next door. "Can I ask you a few questions?"

"You a repo man?"

I took out my bi-fold and held up my star. "Deputy."

"Sure, come on up."

It was always refreshing to meet a member of the public that was willing to talk to law enforcement. His porch looked like it had been built with scavenged wood. I walked up the stairs and opened the door very carefully, afraid that it might just fall off. The old man was seated in a rocker. Up close, I decided that he probably wasn't much over fifty, but a life lived rough had taken its toll.

"Have a seat. I'd stand up, but I just got warm." He smiled at me. The man had fewer teeth than I had fingers.

"I'm Deputy Larry Macklin." Since his hands were under the blankets, I didn't offer to shake.

"Macklin? I thought you was the sheriff."

"That's my father, Ted Macklin," I said. I'd had to explain the relationship between my father and me at least a million times over the years.

"Oh, gotcha, I'm Jeremy Wright. Nice to meet cha'."

"Do you know your neighbor?" I nodded toward the house next door.

"Oh, yeah. That rascal moved in about two months ago. Can't say I'm surprised that a cop is interested in him."

"Why's that?"

"Mean as a snake, a thief, most likely a rapist and an ex-con." He said all of this with great conviction.

"You seem pretty sure."

"I know his type. I've been in prison a couple times

myself. Not for nothin' but drugs and drunk fighting. It's not hard to tell the bad ones. And he's a bad one. Had run-ins with a couple of the folks around here."

"About what?" I took out my pad and pen.

"Tom up the street had a chainsaw go missing. And the Alarcons, they ain't from here, the mister got in a fight with Timberlane about him making comments to his daughter. And she's only fourteen."

"When was this?"

"Not long after Timberlane moved in."

"Any problems since then?"

"What's this all about? He hurt someone?"

"Just the opposite. Someone killed him."

"Good! If I was younger, I'd have roughed him up myself. Never killed no one, but I'd have liked to beat the snot out of that SOB."

"Did he have trouble with anyone else?"

"Now I don't know if I want to help no more. I thought I'd be getting him in trouble and that was all right. Someone killed Timberlane, and he needed killing, well, I don't know if I want to put the heat on them or not."

I thought for a moment what the best approach would be. "What I've learned is that, if a bad guy gets killed, it's most often another bad guy that did it."

He leaned back and thought about it. Finally he said, "True. Well, there was a guy yesterday got in a big fight with Timberlane right in the front yard."

My heart beat a little faster. Maybe this was going to be one of the easy ones. "What did the man look like? Did you know him?"

"Nah, never seen him before. I'd remember if I did. Big old horse of a man. More 'an six feet, maybe six and a half, and no bean pole neither."

"How old was he?"

"Mid-fifties, maybe? Had a ponytail hanging down his back."

"What color was his hair?"

"Light, blondish, think there was some grey in it."

"What kind of clothes was he wearing?"

"What I'd call working man's. Flannel shirt and jean overalls. Nothing new. They were kinda dirty. Oh, yeah, big old work boots."

"Did he come in a car?"

"Older crew cab pickup, think it was a Chevy. Grey. Kind of beat up."

"Didn't happen to see the tag, did you?"

"Nope." Of course I couldn't be that lucky.

"Any other markings on the truck?"

"Not that I saw."

"What did they argue about?"

"Funny about that. They were having like two arguments. On the one hand, Timberlane was all mad about not getting a check or something about being paid, and the big man was mad about some girl."

We needed to backtrack. "Okay, let's start from the beginning. Where were you, and how did this fight start?"

"I was sitting out here. Little warmer yesterday. Anyway, this man, the big one, pulled up in Timberlane's driveway. He got out, went up and knocked on the door. Just like you. Only Timberlane was home. Door opens and the big man stepped back into the yard like he didn't want to go in the house. Timberlane come down and asked something about his money that was owed him. The big man, he pulled out an envelope and tossed it on the ground. Timberlane didn't take too kindly to that. He told him to pick it up. Big man said 'eff you.' Told Timberlane that if he ever saw him again it'd mean a trip to the hospital for Timberlane. Timberlane asked him what his problem was. Big guy says he ought to have Timberlane charged with rape.

"You could see that the big guy was getting more worked up. I thought I was going to see Timberlane get his ass whipped for sure. But I guess he saw the same thing I did. Timberlane said 'screw you' and picked up the envelope, tore it open and looked at what was inside. He shot the big man a bird, but he was backing up toward the house at the same time. Big man just stood there. Then said that if he ever saw Timberlane again he'd do some permanent damage to him. That's the words he used, permanent damage."

"Then the big guy left?"

"Yeah. But he stood outside watching the house for a couple more minutes after Timberlane went inside. Like he was thinking about doing more. But, yeah, he went back to his truck and drove off real fast."

"Nothing else you can remember?"

"No, don't think so."

I got the names and addresses of the other neighbors who'd had encounters with Timberlane, gave Mr. Wright my card and thanked him for his help.

"Don't mind at all. I'm just glad someone got rid of that asshole. Honestly, part of me hopes you don't catch him."

I talked to a couple of the other neighbors and got the same impression of Doug Timberlane. The consensus was that the world was a better place for him being strung up in a tree. I wondered if he had family that might feel differently. I called Pete and got him working on tracking down the owner of the trailer. I needed to get inside and search it. But that could wait. I headed back to the crime scene.

The body had been hauled off by the time I got back. Pete had called in some off-duty deputies and some of our civilian employees to help our crime scene techs search the area for any other evidence.

I caught up with Shantel and she took me to the dead man's effects. I asked her to go ahead and dust his cell phone. After she'd lifted several prints, she handed it to me. Checking it, I saw a number for "Mom." I pressed it.

"David?"

That was weird, but then I remembered the registration of the truck in Timberlane's driveway. I impressed myself by thinking on my feet for a change. "No, I found this phone. I saw the 'Mom' number and thought I might be able to get it back to its rightful owner. Is this David's phone?"

No answer. "Hello?"

There was more dead air and then the connection was broken. Apparently I wasn't fooling anybody. I pushed the button again. She answered but didn't say anything.

"Look, I'm a deputy with the Adams County, Florida Sheriff's Office. You may as well talk to me because if you don't, I'm simply going to use this number to find you."

She said nothing for half a minute, but she didn't disconnect either. Finally, "How'd you get this phone?" The voice was soft and downcast. This was a person who was used to getting bad news.

"I was telling the truth. I found it. Could you give me your name, please?" I had my pad and pen out and leaned on the hood of my car to write.

"Tammy Page. Where did you find it?" A tremor came into her voice.

"Do you have a son, Ms. Page?"

"Yes. Is David all right? Please, is he okay?" Desperation and something else. I think she had been expecting this call for a long time.

"I don't know. We found the phone, but it was in the possession of someone by the name of Doug Timberlane."

"Is he okay?" She was almost yelling now. She hadn't asked who Doug Timberlane was, which led me to one conclusion. I'm not always very good at this detection thing so maybe I was wrong, but it was worth a shot.

"Does your son use the name Doug Timberlane sometimes?"

The question got more of the silent treatment.

"Ms. Page, where do you live?"

"Orlando."

"Is anyone with you?"

"Oh, my God. No! Tell me he's okay. Please." She began to cry.

"Ms. Page, we found the body of a man. The license in

his wallet identified him as Doug Timberlane."

She was just wailing now. There was no point in going on. I told her that I would call back in an hour and hung up.

"Apparently this might not be Doug Timberlane," I said to Shantel. She pulled the dead man's wallet out of the evidence case and we took it apart, dusting the cards and money carefully.

"That answers one question," I said, holding up his license. While it was inside the plastic sleeve it looked real enough to fool me, but without the plastic to obscure the flaws, it was obviously a fake.

There was one card in an interior pocket bearing the name David Tyler. "I think we have a winner. Mom thought it was David calling, and the truck in the driveway was registered to a David Tyler."

Pete and his crew came up with a plastic bin of bagged items that they'd found scattered over an acre around the murder scene. Most of it—cigarette butts, old potato chip bags and odds and ends of clothing—would prove useless. But there was one interesting item—a pay-as-you-go cell phone. If we could find out who purchased it and where, we just might find our killer.

CHAPTER TWO

We finished up and headed back to the office. I ran a check on both names and came up with a long list of priors for David Tyler, stretching back to his eighteenth birthday. I was sure that if his juvie record was unsealed we'd find they went back further.

Looking at the arrest photos for David, I felt confident he was our victim. Though with his record for aggravated assault, sexual battery, sexual assault, lewd behavior, burglary, etc., etc., it was hard to think of him as a victim. He'd spent the majority of his life victimizing others. But you couldn't let the fact that the murdered guy was an asshole affect how hard you hunted for his killer.

I sighed and called his mother again. Bad guys have mothers too.

"Yes?" she answered, sounding bone-weary.

"I'm sorry, Ms. Page. We've looked into the identity of the victim and his real name was David Tyler."

She started to cry, but choked it back. "David is my son."

"You live in Orlando?"

"Sanford, actually." Close enough. "What... what happened to him?" she asked, sounding like she wasn't really sure she wanted to know.

"He was murdered." I didn't want to flood her with all of the horrible details too soon, but she seemed to have found her resolve.

"How was he killed? Have you caught the man who did it?"

"He was hung. And, no, we're just starting our investigation."

"Hung?" She almost laughed, clearly on the edge of hysteria. "I imagined him getting stabbed or shot. The sort of people he called friends... Some of the things he did..." Her voice trailed off. After a moment she asked, "How do I... My son, I want to bury him. How...?"

"We still need to do an autopsy, and we need someone to make a positive identification."

She thought about this for a moment. "I can be there in the morning." Her voice was shaking.

"Do you have someone who can come with you?" I was worried for her. No one should drive in the state that she was in.

"I have to check, but I think my daughter can drive me." I gave her information on places they could stay and which hospital he was at. Adams County is too small to have its own hospital so we use one in Tallahassee. I told her to call me when they were ready and I'd meet them there.

Thinking about the hospital, I looked at my watch and tried to decide if Dr. Darzi had had a chance to do a preliminary exam of the body. What the hell. I dialed his number.

After the usual greetings he said, "Very interesting case." He sounded excited. I took this as a bad sign. I really wanted everything to be cut and dried.

"How so?" I asked.

"He wasn't hung once, but at least five times."

"What?" I wasn't liking this at all.

"The rope left at least five distinct marks on his neck. As though he hung from the rope, then was raised off it, then left to hang again and again."

"Really." I didn't know what to say. My mind was trying to come up with a scenario for the evidence.

"Two of the indentations are very deep. Which one killed him will have to wait for the complete autopsy."

"You sound pretty excited by this. You don't get out much, do you?" I asked good-naturedly.

"What can I say? I get tired of looking at accidents, gunshots and stabbings. This is unique."

"You'd like that, wouldn't you? Get your name in the *Lancet*."

"Not that interesting." He laughed, but I don't think he got my *JAWS* reference.

"So maybe someone had the rope around his neck and dragged him over to the tree before they got it over the branch and pulled him up?"

He thought about that for a moment. "No, I don't think that would account for it. If he'd been struggling while they dragged him to the tree, I would expect the rope marks to be all the way around his neck as he twisted and turned. The rope marks are all on the front of his neck as though he was raised and lowered over and over. You might see this on someone who was standing on their toes, trying not to suffocate. They might rise up for a short period of time, then become exhausted. Let go. Begin to strangle and rise up on their toes again."

"I see. What if someone lifted them up and dropped them? Lifted them and dropped them?" I was thinking of the big guy that Tyler's neighbor had described.

"That would explain it."

He said that the samples had already been sent off for toxicology. We'd get a preliminary report in a couple days and the full results in a couple weeks. He'd perform a full autopsy this afternoon. You could tell he was looking forward to it. I thanked him and disconnected.

As strange as the case was getting, I was grateful that everything might be pointing to one suspect. The big guy. Now all I had to do was find him.

My phone rang. When I saw who it was, my heart jumped. Cara hadn't called me since she'd told me she wasn't comfortable dating a deputy.

"Hey," I said, trying to strike the right tone, somewhere between excited and cool.

"Larry, I need your help. Can you come over to my place?" She sounded very serious. It was clear from her tone that we weren't talking about helping to move a piece of furniture or something equally banal.

"Of course. What's wrong?"

"I'd rather explain it to you in person."

"I'll be there in fifteen minutes."

I had to keep myself from running out of the office, but honestly, everything else was forgotten. We'd only had two dates, but I was enamored with Cara Laursen. She was beautiful, petite and red-haired, a couple years younger than me. But it was much more than her looks. There was a depth to her that I hadn't seen in other women I'd dated. I felt an indefinable connection when I looked into her eyes. It had hit me hard when she told me that my job bothered her.

Oddly, being a deputy had never been important to me. I'd become one for complicated reasons. After my mother died, my dad went into a deep depression. I'd suggested that he run for sheriff. My mom had always joked that he should, since he'd spent his whole career with the department. It seemed like a way to pay tribute to her and to get him out of his depression. He'd agreed on the condition that I become a deputy. And reluctantly, out of love for my father, here I was.

Cara knew that the ties between my father and me were strong and she didn't want to damage them, which just made me respect and care about her more. So for the past few weeks I'd forced myself to give her space, hoping that she felt something for me that would make her reconsider. My pulse quickened as I drove to her duplex.

I restrained myself from running up to her door. It opened as soon as I got within knocking distance. Cara stood in the doorway and it was the first time I'd seen her that she didn't have even a hint of a smile on her face. Alvin, her Pug, ran out and sniffed my ankles as I followed Cara inside.

I almost drew my Glock from its holster when I saw the huge man dominating the small living room. I may not be a great investigator, but even I recognized the large, blond-haired man with a ponytail. I'd found my murder suspect. He looked like a middle-aged Viking, but without the shield or the dragon boat.

I looked from Cara to the man and back. Just then, an older version of Cara walked in from the kitchen. My disorientation must have been clear from my expression. Cara stepped up quickly.

"Larry, this is my father, Henry, and my mother, Anna."

I didn't know whether to shake the huge hand Henry offered or try to cuff him. I settled on shaking his hand as Cara's mother came toward me with outstretched arms. I'm not really a hugger, but she wasn't going to give me an option. I took the hug and gave a little back.

After the greetings we all stood looking at each other. No one seemed to know what to say. Finally Cara offered an explanation.

"My father has a problem." She looked at him. "Dad?"

He sighed. "I saw a dead man this morning," he said without elaborating.

"Look, I've already talked to a neighbor of the dead man who described someone much like yourself arguing with the victim at his house yesterday." I tried for Cara's sake not to sound too accusatory. I was at a loss how to approach this. Anyone else and I'd have already asked them to come down to the sheriff's office to be interviewed, but… it was Cara's dad.

"Yes, that's true. His name was Doug Timberlane. He used to work for us."

That was it? Henry was clearly one of the strong and silent types. I almost blurted out that his name wasn't Doug Timberlane. I had to keep forcing myself to treat Henry as I would any suspect and not give out information that could hurt the investigation.

"Can we sit down?" I looked at Cara. "And I'd like to talk to your father alone."

I saw trust in her eyes and I hoped she could see the same in mine. She turned to her mother. "Mom, why don't we go make something for lunch?"

"Great! We can put out some tabbouleh and hummus and warm up the…" Anna said excitedly as she followed her daughter into the kitchen.

The Viking and I sat across from each other in the living room. His face and hands were weathered from years of working outside. His eyes had a hard, intelligent gaze that was focused on me. This was not the way I wanted to meet Cara's parents.

"Okay. Could you start at the beginning? And give me as much detail as you can." I added the last part hoping to get less laconic statements from him.

He looked up at the ceiling for a moment, apparently deciding where to begin. Or maybe he was trying to figure out how to give more than one sentence answers. "I'm sure Cara's told you about the co-op her mother and I live in down in Gainesville. Well, Doug came to us about five months ago. The co-op has a few trailers for rent. He stayed in one next to another fellow he knew. No one had a problem with him and, about two weeks into his stay, he asked me if we had any work he could do. Most of the folks who live at the co-op help out as a give-a-little/get-a-little deal. But we have a couple positions where we offer a wage. He could handle a backhoe and was mechanically minded, one of our positions was open, so we hired him."

"You hired him or someone else hired him?"

"We have a board, but I'm the manager and they pretty much follow my lead on hiring. I gave him a thumbs up and they agreed."

"Did you check references?"

"He gave me a couple and was upfront about what they were going to tell me. I checked them and, sure enough, they said he worked hard when he was there but had a problem being on time and sometimes he didn't show up at all."

"That didn't bother you?"

"Not really. We pay for the time a person works. If he wants to work two hours one day and ten the next, that's fine. We've had folks with reliability issues in the past, but we work with them. Hell, just about all of us are odd ducks. That's kind of the point of our co-op, for folks who don't conform to society's way of doing things." Henry raised his hand to stop me. "Don't think we're stupid. I Googled his name and checked it against the sex offenders list. We've had some problems like that before."

I had to bite my tongue not to tell him where he went wrong. You aren't going to get the goods if you're checking up on the guy's alias.

"Everything was fine at first. He worked hard. Fixed up a bush hog we were having problems with and dug up and repaired a section of septic lines. Everyone was happy."

"But…"

"We started to get complaints about how he treated some of the women. I talked to him about it and he said he was lonely and hadn't had a girlfriend in a while. I laid down the law to him. He took it well and apologized, saying it wouldn't happen again. And, like I said, I'm not stupid. I didn't just take his word for it that he'd behave. I took some time away from my work to check up on him. Sometimes letting him know I was checking and sometimes doing it as covertly as I could." He stopped and his lips pressed tight. I could tell he didn't want to go on.

"Something happened?"

"A couple of months ago, I stopped in and saw him working on a water line. We talked for a moment, then I told him I had to go make a supply run and asked him if he needed anything. He said he could use another can of PVC glue. No problem. I left, waited fifteen minutes, then came back. I had a ready-made reason. I was going to ask him which of the several different types of PVC glue he preferred.

"When I came around the building—it was one of the units we rent out—I heard a scuffle. What I saw scared the crap out of me. He was holding a young girl, Ellie, by her upper arm, tugging on her. She was fighting him and, just as I came into view, he pulled back his other hand to slap her. He saw me and let go of her, then started to run."

"What'd you do?"

"I caught him."

"And?"

"Took him by the throat and told him I'd strangle him with my bare hands if I ever saw him again. When I dropped him, he took off running. An hour later I checked his trailer. The guy next door said Timberlane had packed his bags and took off. Good riddance, I thought."

That was all well and good but... "So how did you end up here yesterday arguing with him?"

"I guess after a week or so he got his nerve back and started texting me and one or two of the board members whose numbers he had. He wanted his last two weeks pay that he'd earned. At first I just told him to go screw himself, but some of the board members thought we'd be better off if we gave him the money. Well, I finally agreed. When I found out he was living up here, I decided I'd bring him the check instead of sending it."

"Why'd you do that?"

Henry got quiet again. "Two reasons. One, I wanted to give him another warning and, two, well, honestly, I didn't like him living in the same area as Cara. I thought if he knew I knew where he lived, he might decide to move on. I never got the idea he was too attached to any one spot, if you know what I mean."

"You just wanted to warn him? You didn't think that

roughing him up a little might help to move him along?"

"I never intended to harm him."

"Never intended, but did you?"

"No."

"Okay, so why didn't you call the Alachua County Sheriff's Office? He'd assaulted a young girl. You could have had him arrested."

"I screwed up." He held his hands up as if surrendering. "It is a cardinal rule at the co-op that, within reason, we keep our business to ourselves. Our members have some different ideas about pot and other herbs that don't strictly conform to the law. And some of the folks at our place have had some bad experiences with law enforcement. But I'm not making excuses. I made the wrong decision."

Anna came in carrying a plate of pita bread and a bowl of hummus. Cara was right behind her, trying to keep her from interrupting, but it was clear that Anna was a bit of a loose cannon.

"Can I get you two something to drink?" she asked.

"Mom, they want to be left alone to talk for a while."

"Won't hurt them any to have some food and drink."

Why fight it? "Water would be nice."

"Tea, Anna," Henry told her in a gentle voice.

"Be right back." She turned and hurried off. Cara looked at me and shrugged her shoulders as if to say, *I can't control her.*

Henry and I waited for our drinks before going on. Finally Cara managed to herd her mother back out of the room.

"Yesterday. You went out to his place with a check?" I asked.

"Yes. He came out of the house like he was going to give me shit."

"He pissed you off?"

"I couldn't believe his nerve. I threw his check on the ground and told him that I'd kill him if I ever heard that he touched another girl."

23

I had a suspect. He was admitting to a motive. He clearly had the strength to do it, and I was afraid he had the opportunity. But how do you arrest the father of the girl you want to date? "That's all you did, threaten him?"

"Yes. I made a move toward him and he slunk back into the house. So I left."

"If he hadn't retreated?"

Henry looked down at his big hands. I looked at them too. They were huge, callused and could easily be used as weapons. "I would have beat him up. I'm glad he went back inside. I'm not proud that I wanted to hurt him." He looked in my eyes, searching for something. "I'm being honest with you because Cara said I could trust you."

"I appreciate that, and if you had nothing to do with this man's death, I will do everything in my power to make sure you walk away from this unharmed." I was completely sincere. I hoped he could tell that.

"I've had trouble with my anger in the past. Long time ago, before I met Anna." He looked toward the kitchen. "She changed me." He blushed. "And then there was Cara."

"Why were you at the site where he was hanged?" I asked.

He took out his phone and pulled up his recent calls. He held it out to me, showing me a number. I took his phone and pulled mine out, taking a picture of the information displayed on his phone while he talked.

"I got a phone call from that number early this morning. A man's voice said that he needed to talk to me about Timberlane. I started to complain about the time, but he said it was urgent, a matter of life and death. I said okay, and he told me where to go. Cara was up and I asked her if she knew how to get to this place. She said sure and gave me the directions."

"And that led you to the site of the hanging?"

"That was where I saw…" His voice trailed off, his face haunted by the memory.

"Tell me what you saw. What happened?"

"I drove my truck down the dirt road a bit, then stopped and got out. That's when I saw Timberlane hanging from the tree. I ran over there, but it was clear he was dead. I pulled my phone out and was going to call 911, but then I decided I wanted talk to Cara and Anna first. I had just pulled onto the main road when a sheriff's car passed me. I watched in my rearview mirror and saw them turn down the same dirt road I'd just come out of. I knew what that meant."

"What?" If he had this all figured out, he was ahead of me.

"I was being set up. Someone wanted me to be caught with the body."

CHAPTER THREE

I believed almost everything he said and, if he was telling the truth, I was pretty sure his conclusion was right. However, his nemesis had done a pretty damn good job of making a solid case against him. It would be law enforcement malpractice not to take him in for questioning. But I wasn't going to do it. I had no clue what I *was* going to do, but I knew I wasn't going to haul Henry in right then.

"Of course you don't have an alibi for the time of the murder because the call lured you out while the murder took place. You realize how bad this looks?" I asked him.

"It looks that bad because someone intended it to look bad," he said with conviction.

"What will I find if I run your name?"

He sighed heavily. "Nothing for the last thirty years."

"And before then?" I pressed.

"Between the ages of eighteen and twenty I worked as a merchant seaman. I have several charges stemming from bar fights and other... incidents."

"Incidents?"

He was blushing again. "I got in a couple fights over women, mostly." His voice was so low I almost had to ask him to repeat it. "I pled guilty to two of the four charges.

The others were dropped. I spent a total of six months in jail." He stopped talking and looked down at the floor. "What's going to happen now?" he asked, head still down.

I was trying to think of what path I needed to take to ensure that I did my duty and, at the same time, protected Henry as best as I could. "That's what I'm trying to figure out. Why don't you ask Cara and Anna to join us? Whatever happens, it's going to involve everyone."

He got up slowly and left the room. In a moment all three came back. Cara came to my side and put her arm on mine. It was utterly depressing under the circumstances.

"Larry?" Cara asked.

"This doesn't look good," I told her. "But I'm going to figure it out." For encouragement, I added, "We aren't in this alone, either. My dad can be a bit of a horse's ass sometimes, but he's a good man. He'll trust me." I hoped this last part was true. As close as we were, we didn't always see eye to eye.

"But what now?" Cara asked.

"For right now, I just want your dad to stay here. Don't talk to anyone else. I'm going to run the number on the call you got this morning. Maybe we'll get lucky." There were gloomy faces all around. No one believed that the person who went to all this trouble would be so stupid as to use a phone that could be traced back to them. But checking it was something positive that I could do.

"I want you," I pointed at Henry, "to write down everything you remember about all your contacts with Doug. Everything. Who knows what's important and what isn't."

"Why is someone doing these crazy things?" Anna asked in a disillusioned voice. She seemed so naïve for a person of her age.

"I can only see two motivations: to kill Doug and to frame Henry. Which one was the primary objective, I don't know. It's reasonable to think that killing Doug was the main purpose because it seems worse to think that someone would kill a person just so they could frame a third party for the murder. Somehow it seems less callous if they planned on killing Doug and then figured it would be best to frame Henry while they were at it. The bottom line is that it's way too early to know anything. You might want to add to your writing assignment anyone who might hold a grudge against you."

Henry looked genuinely perplexed.

Anna spoke for him. "He gets in some heated arguments, but he always makes amends." She took his arm and hugged it.

"She's taught me to let things go. I apologize and make it right if I fight with someone. I do it sooner than later too."

"But not with Doug?"

"Not with Doug. If you had seen him touching—"

I put my hand up to stop him. "I get it. Just write down everything you can. Don't hesitate to call me if you remember something else or anything happens. I'll be in touch."

Cara walked outside with me. At the car we stopped and just looked at each other. I was trying to find the right thing to say, but she spoke first.

"Thank you. Dad is pretty upset and confused. Honestly, I am too. Who would do this to him?"

The pain in her voice made me want to reach out and hug her, but I was afraid it would just add another layer of emotions that she didn't need right now.

"Cara, I swear to you that I will do everything in my power to get your family through this."

She stepped in and wrapped her arms around me. Women are often braver than men. I hugged her firmly, trying to give her some measure of security and hope. "I'll call you soon," I said, and she gave me a small smile.

Pete called as I was pulling out of Cara's driveway. He'd found the owner of the trailer that Tyler was renting. Turned out it was owned by Justin Thompson, the father of my new and strange confidential informant. Not that I was going to say anything bad about Eddie. Just the month before, my CI had given my dad information that had saved my life.

I told Pete I wanted to drive by the crime scene and that I'd meet him and Thompson at the trailer in an hour.

Crime scene tape was stretched across the dirt road to discourage gawkers. I parked, grabbed a measuring tape and walked down the road to the site of the hanging. The ground was sandy and covered in oak leaves, so we hadn't been able to get any tire tracks. Now I knew that if we had, they probably would have matched Henry's truck.

Walking over to the tree where Tyler had been strung up, I could see the marks on the branch where the rope had scarred the bark. I got down on my hands and knees and felt the ground, moving slowly and carefully toward the spot that was directly under the marks. Eventually, I found what I was looking for—depressions in the dirt, round and about two inches in diameter. There were four of them. They had been partially covered by leaves, but they could still be felt. Taking out my tape, I measured the distance between the impressions.

I was pretty sure now how the murder had taken place. I figured that the killer had forced Tyler to climb up on a stool or a chair, probably at gunpoint. Once Tyler was standing on the stool, the killer threw the rope over the tree branch, made it taut around Tyler's neck, and tied it off. The murderer then removed the stool and replaced it several times, making David Tyler dangle and then regain his purchase, until he finally removed it and let Tyler die.

Why would he remove and replace the stool? Just to torture Tyler? Then a more intriguing thought occurred to me. Maybe he was interrogating Tyler. Asking questions and torturing him when he didn't get the answers he wanted. Knowing that Tyler was a criminal, maybe he had stolen something of the killer's. Could it be drug related?

But none of that answered the question of why the killer wanted to involve Henry. Just to throw us off the scent?

That seemed a little far-fetched. How did the killer even know about Henry? Maybe he was watching Tyler's house, saw Henry get in a fight with him, and came up with the plan to frame him on the fly. But then how would he get Henry's phone number? Probably from Tyler while he was torturing him.

My theory made a lot of sense. I turned it around in my head, trying to find a flaw in my logic. It seemed like the simplest explanation. If Occam's razor held true, that should be the solution. *Hey, I'm getting better at this,* I thought. Now all I had to do was find the killer and Henry would be off the hook.

Twenty minutes later I pulled into the driveway of the trailer. Pete was already there. I looked over and saw the old man sitting on his porch next door. I waved, but he didn't wave back. Probably asleep. The day had warmed up to the point that it was perfect napping weather. I thought about checking to see if he was alive and figured that was silly.

"Thompson should be here shortly. Said it would take him a little while to go home and get the key," Pete said without looking up from his phone. I nodded and left him leaning against his car while I walked around the trailer again. *How much could Thompson be charging for this dump?* I wondered.

I heard a car park at the curb. With Tyler's, Pete's and mine, there wasn't room for another vehicle in the driveway. I saw a lean man of average height get out of a newish SUV. He was wearing jeans and cowboy boots, but it looked more like a costume than a working man's outfit.

"Justin Thompson," he said without putting out his hand.

"I'm Deputy Macklin and this is Deputy Henley," I said.

Thompson squinted at us as though he was trying to decide if we were worthy of committing to memory. "You're the sheriff's son," he said, giving me a double dose of his squinty eyes.

"That's right." I stared back at him. My CI had told me

how this man had treated him when he discovered that Eddie was a cross-dresser, which could be summed up as mean and nasty. I had no doubt that Eddie was telling the truth. Justin Thompson looked like a man that could strangle babies for fun.

"I knew he was a little shit when I rented it to him," Thompson said, digging a set of tagged keys out of his jacket pocket. "But what are you going to do? I ran a credit check on him and it came back clean."

David got a lot of mileage out of that fake ID, I thought. Pete and I put on gloves. I took the key from Thompson and opened the door.

Inside, the house smelled of stale beer and cigarette smoke. Thompson went around opening blinds and turning on lights. "Shit, it'll take a week to get this place clean," he said, looking at the mess that Tyler had left him.

Thompson watched us go through the living/dining/kitchen area of the trailer. There was trash, lots and lots of trash. Beer cans and bottles, pizza boxes and bags from every fast food place in the county. We found his keys, which reinforced the idea that he hadn't left on his own. Was David abducted from inside the trailer or had he met the murderer at the door and been ordered into a car? Looking around, there was no way to tell if there had been a struggle. But the killer had to have been here, which made this a crime scene.

"We need to let our crime scene techs go over the trailer," I told Thompson.

"How long will it take? I'd like to clean it out and get it rented again as soon as possible."

"We don't intend on dragging our feet. They'll come out tomorrow, and if we don't find any blood or obvious trace evidence, you should be able to get back inside in a couple of days."

Thompson looked like he was considering this. I wanted to tell him this was not optional and if he wanted me to make it longer, I could, but I didn't want to start a fight with the man.

"Yeah, okay," he allowed.

The sun was going down as we finished. I looked at my watch. It was five-thirty. Ivy was going to wonder where I was. Not that she'd gone out this morning. She'd sniffed the cold air and decided that staying inside, cuddled up in warm blankets, was where a tabby cat should be on a frosty winter morning.

I considered going by Dad's house, but I was exhausted and didn't want to have to decide whether to tell him about Henry or keep it from him. Being sheriff meant that he had higher priorities than protecting the feelings of my would-be girlfriend.

So I went straight home and fed Ivy. She always seemed grateful that I'd rescued her from the parking lot of the sheriff's office. She'd been living off scraps given to her by burly deputies who would have been embarrassed if anyone had seen them calling "kitty, kitty" to her.

After a hot bath and an hour with social media, I called it a night. I always slept well in my trailer in the woods. It had been part of the twenty acres when I bought the land five years ago. I had a place picked out to build a house if I ever managed to save up the money, but for now, I'd still rather live in a trailer in the woods than a mansion in the city.

CHAPTER FOUR

Rain was pounding on the roof when I got up in the morning. The Internet said that a front was moving through and we'd have falling temperatures by evening and a hard freeze tomorrow.

"Looks like another day inside for you, little girl," I told Ivy. She took it well as she kneaded a blanket on the couch and prepared to sleep the day away.

I remembered that Tammy Page was going to be in town today. Why did it always rain when I had to meet a family at the morgue? As if things weren't depressing enough.

I got to the office and went through the reports on my desk. There were three new ones from the night before. I looked over at Pete's desk. There were only two sitting there. He wasn't in yet. His morning routine called for a huge breakfast at Winston's Grill. No one said a word to him about coming in late because, the truth was, he got a ton of useful information gabbing with the locals every morning. We'd all benefited from gossip he had heard while slurping down pancakes and bacon. Police work comes in many forms.

Now I wistfully fantasized about dropping one of my cases onto his pile. But Lt. Johnson had already assigned them electronically. No chance I'd get away with it.

Two of my new cases were domestic assaults. I had a hard time with domestics. I always wanted to slug the abuser and shake the victim and ask them why they put up with it. Of course, relationships are complex and some people are more emotionally able to deal with life than others. And, yes, I'd had a psychology course that talked about codependence and the power dynamics in abusive relationships. But I still had a hard time understanding it at a gut level.

The new cases were both first-time reports at those addresses and both involved people under thirty. Maybe I could talk to the victims and get them to understand that they would be doing the abuser a favor by pressing charges. If the abuser got help now, maybe they could find new ways of dealing with their emotions that would change their lives. Or not. This was one of the reasons I had a hard time fully committing to being a law enforcement officer; most of the time it felt like I was just beating my head against the wall.

The other case was a hit and run. Damage to a car parked on the street. The rub was that someone had been sitting in the car and ended up with a broken nose when the other car rear-ended them. They got a brief look at the car, but couldn't give much of a description. The officer had called the crime scene techs out and they'd gotten some transfer paint samples off of the damaged car and pictures of skid marks. I'd have to do a little work on this one.

I'd finished going through my emails when my phone rang. It was Tammy Page. I told her where to meet me at the hospital in Tallahassee and said I'd be there within the hour.

It was still raining as I got out of my car and walked up to the front entrance of the hospital. I only had to wait a few minutes when I saw a short, stout woman walking across the parking lot with her head held up, looking straight ahead and not seeming to notice the rain pounding down. A younger version of the woman walked beside her, head down and guiding her mother around the puddles. Once they were under shelter, the daughter tried wiping some of the rain off of her mother.

I introduced myself.

"I'm Alice and this is my mother, Tammy."

Tammy Page stared straight at me. "I want to see him. Alice doesn't think I should, but I do."

Alice sighed dramatically. "Mother, why put yourself through more pain for that boy?"

Her mother looked at her reproachfully and the younger woman rolled her eyes in defeat.

"Well, let's get on with it then," Alice said to me.

I led them through the corridors and down the elevator to the morgue. I'd called ahead to make sure that the body was ready and presented as compassionately as possible. Tammy would have nothing to do with the viewing room and insisted on going in to stand next to her son. She touched his cheek, ignoring the purple color and puffed up features.

I took them to sign the necessary papers, then we retreated to a small room near the hospital security office so I could ask them a few questions. I'd thought about talking to mother and daughter separately, but I wanted to see how they interacted and how they each reacted to the other's opinions and thoughts about Tyler's murder.

"I know he was in trouble a lot. Was there a particular reason that he'd chosen to live under an alias at this time?"

"I don't know," his mother said.

"He was a criminal. I'm sure that he was running from something or someone. He hurt a lot of people. Honestly, I don't care if you ever catch the person who did this," the daughter blurted.

"Alice!" her mother chastised her.

"Mother, he never did anything but cause you pain and grief. For God's sake, for once see him like he was, not the way you wanted him to be."

"He's dead, can't you leave him alone now?"

"Quit defending him and I'll quit attacking him. He was a horrible person."

This wasn't getting us anywhere. "Are there other brothers and sisters?"

"No, he was my first and Alice is my youngest."

"He was my half-brother," Alice said flatly, trying to distance herself from a man she clearly despised.

"I was married to David's father, Charles Tyler, for two years. He beat me and made threats at David, so I left."

"And the nut didn't fall far from the tree," his sister said, completely missing the irony that her brother had been hung from a tree. The hatred that Alice had for David was almost a physical presence in the room. I didn't think it could all be accounted for by his abuse of his mother's good nature. I decided to take her aside later and ask her about it.

"When was the last time that either of you had contact with David?"

"He called me about two weeks ago. He needed money and I sent it to him."

"Ha!" Alice huffed. "When *didn't* he need money?"

"Those people at that commune fired him and didn't give him his severance pay. I told him he should talk to them and make them pay him what they owed him."

"He didn't tell you why they asked him to leave?" I asked.

"The people running the place were upset that David was pointing out all the things that needed to be repaired. He didn't like to see people being taken advantage of. He said that some of the houses didn't even have decent plumbing."

Boy, I thought, *she really drank the Kool-Aid.*

"Jeez, Mom, you don't believe that crap, do you?"

"I know David had problems. But all of it wasn't his fault."

"When was the last time that you heard from your brother?" I said, trying to redirect Alice.

"Ten years ago. Maybe longer."

"Do either of you know of someone who might have done this to David?"

"No. He got in arguments and had problems with people, but I can't imagine anyone doing something like *this*," Tammy choked out.

I caught Alice's eye. She looked like she had plenty more to say on the subject, but she seemed to realize that this wasn't the time to pile more on her mom.

"That's enough for now. Let me walk you all back to your car."

It had stopped raining by the time we got outside. The wind was beginning to shift from the north, bringing a bitter bite to the damp air. When we reached their car, I held the door open for Tammy. Once she was inside I turned to Alice, who was standing by the driver's door. "I'd like to talk to you alone." I handed her my card.

"It would be my pleasure," she said with a nod. "Let me take Mom for lunch and get her settled back in the hotel. We're staying the night."

"Call me, anytime this afternoon will work. Do you mind driving over to Adams County?"

"Actually, an excuse to get away from Mom for a little while would be great."

I watched her get in and drive off. One bad child can do so much harm to a family.

A text from Dad arrived on my phone as I got in my car. He wanted to see me in his office. Wondering what he wanted, I replied I'd be there in an hour. Had he found out about Henry? Did he know I was treating a suspect more like a victim? I doubted it. Who else knew? I hadn't even filled Pete in on all the developments. I felt a little guilty about leaving them out in the wind, but until I had an alternative to Henry, I wanted to keep things close.

As soon as I entered Dad's office, I knew that I was screwed. He looked up and smiled at me. Usually he just sat behind his Texas-sized desk and puttered with the computer or case files while he mumbled at me. A smile meant he wanted something.

He was tall from the waist up so he looked bigger than his 5'10" when he was seated. His ball cap with *Sheriff* written in large orange letters sat on the edge of his desk. His hair was thinning, white and often a bit unruly, but he seemed to like showing it off, taking his cap off every chance he got.

"Son, have a seat."

I sat down, knowing full well that I was falling into a trap. "What do you want?" I asked bluntly.

"Come on, now. Would a little small talk between a father and son be such a bad thing?"

Oh, my God. It must be really bad. "I guess not," I answered, waiting for the trap to snap closed.

"How's that case coming? The guy found hanging?" He sounded engaged and interested. I tried to remember how often that had happened.

"Pretty good. I think I understand it. Someone wanted something from our victim. I don't think it's drug related. We found some recreational drugs in his apartment, but nothing much, and he was broke for all practical purposes. Might be a gambling debt. Something like that." Of course I left off the whole part about the killer trying to frame my girlsomething's father.

"Well, I'm sure you'll get a handle on it. Got that paperwork done on the Kemper case?"

I had to put together a pile of reports and evidence receipts for the prosecutor on the case that almost got me killed. "I'll have it to him by Tuesday of next week."

"Excellent. I never have to worry about you doing your paperwork. Next week. That reminds me, I have that sheriff's conference to go to."

Oh, Lord, now I knew where this was going.

"But I have a little bit of trouble with my babysitter. He has to go out of town. I've got a neighbor looking after the horses, but you know Mauser can't be left with just anyone. So I'll need you to watch him for a few days."

Mauser was Dad's one-hundred-and-ninety-pound, black-

and-white monster of a Great Dane. He was going on two years old with no manners whatsoever. Dad was the world's worst dog trainer. He was inconsistent, failed to set boundaries, failed to reward good behavior and, last but not least, seemed to find Mauser's destructive and dangerous behavior hilarious.

"How long?"

"Not long, just Thursday through Sunday."

"That is an eternity with that dog."

"Come on now. He's just a puppy," he said. I bit down hard on my tongue rather than get into the usual argument about Dad's non-existent training techniques.

"You know, I have a job too. What am I going to do with him during the day Thursday and Friday?"

"I give you permission to bring him to work. Everyone here loves the big goof."

Dad obviously hadn't heard what some of the people in the office had to say about the canine menace. True, there were about half a dozen folks who were as smitten with the oaf as Dad was, but there was at least one guy who preferred to take personal days off rather than be in the same building with Mauser.

"And I'm on call Saturday night." We split the night shift between a few investigators and supervisors.

"Not anymore." He made a note. "I'll call Lt. Johnson as soon as we're done. You can take your shift on Wednesday night."

There was nothing I could say. Dad had put me in this position before and I still hadn't found a way to get out of it. Putting my foot down *was* an option, and honestly Dad wouldn't give me that much grief about it. However, he was a master at passive resistance and he'd find a dozen ways to make me feel like crap if I refused. It simply wasn't worth it. I couldn't even use Ivy as an excuse since the darn cat was one of Mauser's biggest fans. I think she liked the fact that he always found ways of getting food and spreading it around the house. Whatever. I was alone in this battle and I always lost.

"Make my shift on Tuesday night. If I'm going to get Mauser on Thursday, I'll need a good night's sleep Wednesday."

"Done. Good man." He made a note about the shift. "Come by Thursday morning about nine. And keep me informed on the murder." And that was it. He waved me off. Dazed at the turn of events, I walked out of the office.

CHAPTER FIVE

Back at my desk I tried not to dwell on the nightmare I faced next week. It was Friday and I wanted to clear up a few more things before I left.

I closed out the two domestics. I'd talked to the victims in each case, and they both agreed to press charges, so the files could be turned over to the prosecutor's office. It was about three when I looked up from my computer to see Alice Page standing there.

"I thought I'd just come by," she said.

I stood up. "Great, glad you did." I led her to the small conference room outside of Dad's office and we sat down across from each other.

"I was getting the impression you had a little more to say about your brother than you wanted to in front of your mother," I prodded her.

"Half-brother," she repeated, then fell silent as if gathering strength to say something. I waited. "He was evil. The worst human being I ever knew," she said sincerely.

"Why do you say that?" That seemed a little strong. I'd seen a lot of creeps and his record didn't look as bad as a lot of them.

"He raped me." She choked back tears. "I am sooo glad

that he is dead. I've wanted to see him punished for all the nasty, vile things he did to me and others for twenty years. But he said he'd hurt me if I told anyone." She was almost hyperventilating. "My only regret is that I didn't do it. At the very least, I wish I could have seen him dangling from that rope."

I almost offered to go get the crime scene photos for her. "When did he rape you?"

"Started when I was thirteen."

"I'm sorry. Have you told your mother?"

"I've tried to several times. I was twenty the first time I tried to explain why I couldn't stand to be in the same room with David. But she didn't hear me. It was like her mind refused to even take it in, let alone process it."

"That must have been awful for you." I couldn't imagine what she must have endured.

"Those events shaped my entire life. I'm a psychologist. I lived with all that pain and now I try to help others. What's sad is how often I fail. Too many people are damaged so badly that they can't be healed."

"You sound like you've been able to create a life apart from what David inflicted on you."

"You have to try, right?"

"You realize that no matter how terrible your half-brother was, I still have to do my best to find his killer?"

"I realize that someone who takes the law into his own hands is wrong. I know that's true, but there is a big part of me that would like to shake the hand of the murderer. I don't know why he did it and I understand it was wrong. But I think I would have killed him myself years ago if I'd had the guts. Whoever hung David up by the neck did me a great service. The moment that Mom told me he was dead, I felt like a giant cross had been lifted off my shoulders."

"Is there any point in me asking if you know of anyone who might have done this to David?"

"I don't know. Would I tell you if I did? Luckily that's not a decision I have to make."

"Anything you could tell me about David's recent past would be a help."

"I've tried to avoid even hearing his name during the last decade. I have no idea who he was involved with. There were girls when I was growing up that I think he did things to, but I couldn't say for sure. I can tell you, both as a psychologist and as a person who knew David, he hadn't changed. I don't think he could have changed. That means that there are other women and girls that he harassed and probably raped."

I wanted to ask her why she didn't try harder to get him put away. But she had suffered enough and I could see in her eyes that she hated the fact she hadn't been able to stop him.

"Thank you for coming and talking to me," I said sympathetically.

"I didn't do it for you or for David. I did it for me." She got up and walked out.

I finished up some more paperwork and when I looked up it was after five. Matt Greene was the only other investigator still in the office. He glanced at me as I stood up and put on my coat. Matt had the personality of a badger, which as a colleague made him hard to deal with, but also made him a tough and tenacious investigator. We had never gotten along. He resented my family ties with the sheriff and I didn't like the fact that he was an ass. However, after being forced to work together on the Kemper case, we'd come to something approaching mutual respect.

"Got another murder?" He managed to say it with only a hint of envy.

"Yes." I wasn't sure that I wanted to engage him in conversation.

"Heard they found the victim hanging from a tree on the south side. At least it wasn't racial." Hearing him echo my first thoughts made me feel a little of the thin blue line's kinship with him.

"Yeah, it would have been a whole different animal. But it looks like he was killed by a colleague who wanted something from him."

"Robbery?"

"The victim didn't have anything."

"Drugs?"

"Possibly. The guy was a nasty piece of work, but he looked to be only a recreational drug user."

"First time try at running drugs and he tries to double-cross the buyer?"

"Maybe, but if so we haven't found any evidence."

"You get stuck, I'll be glad to take a look at it. Did you get your paperwork done for the prosecutor?" He had his own set of reports to turn in on the Kemper case.

"I've promised them to him by Tuesday."

"I turned mine in yesterday." He turned back to his monitor. "Going over a couple of cold cases." He didn't look back at me. What did I expect? He wasn't going to develop people skills overnight.

"Have a good weekend," I told him and left.

When I got home I called Cara.

"Dad's going a little crazy. He can't stand to be away from the co-op for too long. And Mom is driving me insane. When do you think they can go back to Gainesville?"

"I'm sorry, but probably not before Tuesday. I want to get all the preliminary lab reports back and follow up on the phone call your dad got. We found a phone at the murder site, a pay-as-you-go model that had been recently activated. The number matches the one used to call your dad. The company is tracking the number and should be able to tell me where it was purchased on Monday."

"I got Dr. Barnhill to let me work Saturday and do the dog walking on Sunday, just so I have an excuse to get out of the house. Maybe I can put Dad to work in the backyard or something."

"I'd like to say that he can go now, but…"

"No, I understand, you have to do your job," Cara said, trying to reassure me. I hated for her to see this as another example of my job being an issue. "You've been a big help. My dad wouldn't have done well if some cop had dragged him into the station and started questioning him. I know you've done us a huge favor. I'd just forgotten what it's like to live with my parents. Love them, but they can drive me nuts."

"Hang in there. I'll call you as soon as I know something."

Ivy bumped my hand as I hung up. "I hope you're happy. Your boyfriend is coming to visit next week. Any damage that lunk of a dog does is on your head," I told her as she settled in my lap, ignoring my complaints.

CHAPTER SIX

I went back to the office on Saturday to take care of the hit-and-run report. I called the victim and was told pretty much exactly what was in the report. Still, you have to follow up. Some of the deputies are great at doing most of the He-Man aspects of law enforcement, but are a bit lacking in their basic math and English skills.

This isn't always true. For instance, I always look forward to Deputy Mark Edwards's reports. He themes them. Some are done as a comedy of errors while others are Gothic tragedies. We've actually shared his reports around the office.

Edwards was one of those people who got into law enforcement because he wanted to help people, and he'd managed to keep his sense of humor and good nature throughout all the horrors and filth that you have to deal with out on the road. People who paint officers as all one color are missing the complexities that drive people to enter the job. Every deputy and police officer has their own reasons for joining. For many, their reasons are noble—to help others, to uphold the standards of our communities, to provide for their families while protecting others.

My phone rang. Glancing at the ID I saw that it was

Eddie, my first official confidential informant. I sighed and answered the call.

"Hey, Eddie."

"You almost sound glad to hear from me."

"Yeah, sure, if you say so. What's up?"

"I need to meet with you." Since hooking up with him a month ago, I'd learned that "meet up" was code for "I need money."

"What's it about?"

"Not on the phone." *Of course not, I can't give you money over the phone*, I thought. But I chided myself. The man *had* saved my life.

"Okay. The usual?" The usual was Rose Hill Cemetery.

"Yeah, in an hour?"

"I'll see you there."

Eddie was waiting for me when I reached the north side of the graveyard. I got out of my car and we walked over to lean against the wall. The air was frigid, but the wall provided some relief from the wind.

Rose Hill was the second oldest cemetery in Adams County. It was started in 1840 during a yellow fever outbreak. Against the north wall were the graves of Union soldiers killed during the Civil War. The joke was that it was as far north as they could bury them and still be in the cemetery. There were over a hundred of the two-foot-high, rounded white gravestones. War dead are always humbling. So many giving their lives for causes that most of them were too young to understand.

"What's going on?" I asked.

Eddie looked more nervous than usual, which was saying something. "I want you to know that things have worked out just the way I said. My cousin has been inviting me to his place, and they're treating me like a regular since we took out the competition."

The first tip he'd given me was on one of his cousin's competitors in the drug business. He'd sold it to me as a way for him to make points with his family, which would provide him with the opportunity to learn more and feed me more information.

"That's great. I'm really thrilled that I've been able to help you get back into your family's good graces," I said sarcastically. "Which reminds me. I saw your dad the other day."

His eyes narrowed and a scowl came across his face. "Screw that. I got something for you."

"Waiting."

"Okay, I was at a party with my cousins and I heard them talking. They were saying they needed some security for Saturday night."

"Tonight?"

"Yeah."

"When was this party?"

"Thursday, no, Wednesday night."

"And you're just now telling me about this?"

"I'm using again." He looked down at the grave in front of him. "I scored and got pretty messed up. But you're missing the point."

"What is the point? They need security. For what? A wedding? A concert? One of their drug dens?"

"No, see, they were talking about a shipment coming in from Tampa. So the security is for the hand-off."

"Okay. Do you know where this hand-off is happening?"

"Yeah, I do, but you still don't see."

Okay, maybe I was being a little dense, but he was right. I didn't see what he was driving at.

"When they say security, they mean a cop. One of the guys they got on payroll."

I stood up straight, very interested now. Eddie had used the specter of bad cops and, more precisely, a bad deputy to pull me into this CI/investigator relationship. But until now he'd been cagy about putting me onto the bad cops. His family was one of the largest and oldest in the county, and they had relatives in Calhoun's police department and one in ours, but he swore they were not the cops on the payroll. I knew that some parts of the family had nothing to do with other parts, so I was willing to keep an open mind.

"So you're saying that at this hand-off they will have a dirty cop making sure things don't go south."

"Yeah, that's what I said." He gave me a look like I was stupid.

"Watch yourself. Now where is this going to take place?"

"No, look, this is an opportunity for you to see who the dirty cop is, but you can't bust anybody. If you do that, they might be able to trace it back to me."

"I'm good with that," I said rather cruelly.

"Hey, that hurt. Remember I—"

"Yes, you saved my life when you texted my dad the location where the bad guy was holding me, blah, blah, blah. Which I really appreciate, by the way. And I also get that if we put them on alert, everyone will get paranoid and we could lose the opportunity to ferret out the other rotten apples."

"Okay, you ain't completely stupid." I motioned like I was going to slug him and he dodged me. "Sorry, sorry, just kidding, cool it. Do we have an understanding?"

"Yes."

"Say it, man."

"I'll just observe and not move in and make arrests." I had to admit that he was probably right that the best thing to do was observe and take names. Finding the bad cops was my top priority. Well, actually, my top priority was finding the rotten deputy. For any number of reasons, I didn't want a crook in our department. Not the least of which was to protect Dad. Any scandal in the sheriff's office would reflect on him. With an election coming up next year, he didn't need any bad news making its way to the papers.

"The deal is going down behind Jimmy's 4x4 in the industrial park."

I knew the area pretty well. The industrial park was on the west side of town near the interstate, just up the road from the AmMex Trucking Company.

"What time?"

"Ahhh, I'm a little fuzzy on that. I can't remember exactly. I think it was like one or midnight."

"You don't know what time? Oh, I guess I can understand that, one sounds so much like midnight! Damn it, Eddie."

"It was a party, there was a lot of noise, and they weren't talking to me. 'Sides, I couldn't ask them to repeat it, now could I?" he said.

From reading history, I knew that intelligence was seldom very intelligent. You had to take what you got and make the most sense out of it that you could. "Okay, Eddie, think. Are you sure that it was between midnight and one o'clock. Not later?"

He got a thoughtful expression on his face. "Yeah, pretty sure. And these guys aren't going to be doing anything any later than two in the morning."

Assuming that they weren't complete idiots, he was probably right about that too. Eleven to one is the best time to be out on the streets since there are not a lot of people, but not so few that anyone driving around would draw attention. In a rural county like ours, after one o'clock in the morning, any car driving around stands out. There isn't anything open, so if law enforcement sees a car they get interested. Around five, a few early birds get up and start heading to work and by then all the bad guys are burned out from the night before. Between one and five in the morning are the golden hours for catching drunks, burglars and other miscreants who are up to no good.

"Okay. I'll check it out."

"Hey, man, could you lend me a little?"

I gave him my *what the hell* expression.

"Seriously, I got to buy gas and stuff."

I took out my wallet and gave him two twenties. "Don't snort it, stick it in your arm or do anything else stupid with it."

He looked properly chagrined. "No, I got to get straight

again. Thanks," he said, looking at the money like it was the best gift anyone had ever given him.

Damn it all, I always walked away feeling sorry for him.

After leaving the cemetery I made a quick swing by the industrial park, scoping out a good spot to hide and observe the action that night. Then I went back to the office, checked my email and worked on the files for the Kemper case. By two o'clock I'd managed to fill a plastic box with all the reports and evidence logs that the prosecutor had asked for. Another check of my email brought up a message from the company that made the phone we'd found near Tyler's body. According to them, the phone had been bought at the Fast Mart on Jefferson Street on Tuesday. With luck, maybe they'd have a CCTV image of the killer. I grabbed my coat and headed for the door. A lot of these small stores had a system where the footage would be replaced with new footage every couple of days, so time could be important.

The Fast Mart was not the gold standard of quicky-marts. It was on the edge of one of the worst neighborhoods in Calhoun. A couple of fellows who'd been loitering out front shuffled off when they saw me drive up. As I entered the store, a bell over the doorway gave a clang that was meant to alert the clerk. It wasn't needed. The young black man behind the counter was staring at the door, looking relieved to see me.

He peered past me out the front window. "You a cop?"

"Sheriff's deputy."

"Those guys gone?"

I backed up and looked outside. "They're gone."

"Damn it, they're going to think I called you."

"Is that a problem?"

He looked at me wide-eyed as he realized he'd said too much. "Ah, no." He was visibly shaking.

I took a closer look at him. He was clearly not the tough guy you'd want working behind a counter in this part of town.

"You new to this area?"

"Man, I work for the owner at one of his stores in Tallahassee. He asked me to fill in over here for a few days. But this shit is bad."

"Those two guys were dealers," I told him.

"I asked them to leave earlier and one of them showed me a knife and said that if I didn't like working here, they could make sure I didn't ever have to work in Calhoun again. He was serious! Damn it. The boss looked at me and thought I'd fit in over here. He's crazy." The young man, who couldn't have been more than twenty, was pacing up and down behind the counter. "I'm from Naples, man."

"You need to call your boss and tell him you're out of your element over here," I told him.

"Man, I don't know. I can't just run out on him."

"Listen to me. I need to look at your security footage from a few nights ago. The store has CCTV, right?"

"That's the only thing that works around here," he said, still paying more attention to his dilemma than to me.

"You let me see that tape and I'll fix things with your boss. At least I'll get you out of here today. What you decide to do beyond that is up to you."

"Okay, sure, it's in the back," he said without hesitation.

"Go lock the front door and then take me in back and show me where it is."

Sure enough, the store had a pretty sophisticated recording and monitoring system set up. "It's the same as the one we have at the store in Tallahassee," the clerk said. "What day do you want to see?"

"Back it up to Tuesday."

He showed me how the search function worked and how to play, rewind and fast-forward. I sent him back out front and went through the tape. Most of it I could watch at fast-forward. The pre-pay phones were on a rack in front and to the right of the cash register, so all I had to do was watch for someone reaching for one of the phones. They sold three of them. I was disappointed to see that the last one was bought by David Tyler on Tuesday morning. He used a mix of coins and bills to pay for it. Cleary this was not someone who had stolen a lot of money or drugs.

I called the clerk back and had him show me how to make a copy of the video. He had to use a thumb drive he got from his car, so I paid him for it.

"Do you want to go home?" I asked him.

"I'm going to get shot I if stay here. But how—"

I put my hand up and stopped him, then I called a friend of mine at the fire station. Great thing about fire stations is that there are always people hanging around. "I'm at the Fast Mart on Jefferson. Any chance one of you could come out and find some fire violations and shut it down for a day?" They were delighted to help.

"I'd suggest you explain to your boss that the color of your skin doesn't indicate the type of people you're used to dealing with."

He looked like he was going to cry when he thanked me. Being a clerk at some of these stores was more dangerous than being a cop. At least we were armed and trained to deal with crooks and drug dealers.

CHAPTER SEVEN

I went home to feed Ivy, grab a bite for myself and decide what I was going to do that night. Going out to the industrial park without telling anyone would be stupid. But who could I tell, and how much should I tell them? Who was easy: Pete.

"Hey," I said when he picked up the phone.

"It's Saturday," he groaned.

"Where's Sarah?"

"How'd you know that she's not here?"

"Because you weren't looking for a diversion. If she was there you'd be thrilled that I called."

"Ha, got me. She's with her sister and the girls shopping. God save me from the holidays. I was just sitting here watching the TV and drinking my third beer. And you know what? No one told me it was my third beer. I have hours until the mall in Tallahassee closes. Heaven. But do I get left in peace? No, my partner has to call. So what do you want?"

"Something simple, nothing that will upset your evening of sloth and gluttony. I just wanted to let you know that I'm going to check out a hunch at the industrial park."

"What's out there? And why don't you call dispatch and let them know?"

"My CI told me there might be something going down

out there tonight. It may not be anything, so I want to keep it hush-hush." I could almost hear the gears in his head working.

"You know if I hadn't had a few beers, I'd insist on going out there with you?"

"I know that and if I thought I needed you, I'd have given you the heads-up earlier."

"Wait a sec." I heard him groan as he raised his bulk out of his recliner. "Okay now." I knew he'd gotten a pen and paper to make notes. If something did happen, he didn't want to rely on a fuzzy conversation that he had just before dozing off in front of the TV. Pete didn't look like much of a cop, but once you scratched the surface you found a professional law enforcement officer who took his job a lot more seriously than some of the hotshot SWAT team heroes.

He tried one more time to talk me into getting some backup. I assured him that I'd have my radio and phone with me if I needed assistance in a hurry.

I packed a stakeout bag with PowerBars, water, binoculars and a flashlight. In my trunk there was a rifle and shotgun. I had my Glock and a couple extra magazines. I attached a rail light to my handgun. All of this seemed like overkill, but I wanted to be prepared. The possibility of facing drug dealers and bad cops called for some extra precautions. I also got my digital camera that had a pretty good lens and would take better pictures in low light than my phone could. I put on a couple layers of clothes, starting with a pair of flannel underwear. The temperature would be around freezing by midnight. I would have gone and checked out some infrared and night-vision surveillance equipment, but that would have involved filling out forms. We were a small department and that stuff was still expensive. I'd have had an easier time getting one of the department's M4 machine guns than the expensive optics.

At ten-thirty I told Ivy I'd be back in four hours and left the house. Outside in the cold and the dark, I wondered if I was crazy to listen to Eddie. But he'd never told me anything that wasn't true. At least, not anything that I could check. Now whether or not he'd heard his cousin correctly at a party when they were all a little high, that was a different question. I sighed. *Doesn't matter because I'm committed now*, I thought as I got into my car.

I got there by eleven. There was no one in the front of the industrial park as I drove by. I turned around and came back. I didn't dare drive back in the park and onto the circle where Jimmy's 4x4 was. If someone was back there waiting and watching, it would be a dead giveaway. The only thing I could do was to put my car in the woods close to the entrance and see who came and went. Hopefully I would recognize any cop who was with them. I pretty much know every deputy and police officer in the county by sight. There are only about thirty-five deputies and a dozen police. The only thing that might have screwed it up was if I couldn't recognize their car or see them through their windshield.

I backed my car in farther than I'd planned. I wanted to make sure that I wasn't seen. A dirt path allowed me to park far enough back in the woods that someone could pull partway up the path and still not see me in the dark. The downside was that I couldn't see anything from inside my vehicle. I needed to be outside and lying on the ground closer to the entrance.

After parking, I took a green army blanket from my trunk and walked closer to the road. I found a small depression where I could lie down, cover myself with the blanket and be reasonably well concealed. As an extra measure of camouflage, I threw leaves and sticks on the blanket. They stuck well to the thick wool knap. By eleven-fifteen I was down on the ground and well hidden. That's when the first ant bit me. Five minutes later I had shaken all the ants off me and managed to get resituated four feet to the right of my first position.

Midnight came and went. My neck was sore and I was just barely avoiding hypothermia. Just as I was trying to decide when I would give up, the first vehicle, an SUV, pulled into the industrial park. I'd gotten lucky because Industrial Drive was higher than the main road, so cars had to slow to make the approach. The county had also put in half a dozen streetlights at the entrance so I would get a pretty good look at the occupants of each car as they came in.

The SUV looked local, but I didn't recognize anyone on the passenger side of the car. Even with the streetlights, the people on the driver's side were hard to see. The second vehicle to arrive was an upscale crew cab truck. Its tinted windows didn't allow me to see anyone, but I was guessing it was with the SUV. The buyers had shown up first, which made sense since it was their home ground.

I shifted a little to get the feeling back in my lower legs. Just as I resettled, I saw another car pull in. It didn't go into the industrial park. Instead it turned around quickly and backed down the dirt path I was parked on. My heart was trying to pound its way through my chest as I watched the car get closer and closer to where I lay. I was frozen in place. I thought about running, but it was too late to get my car out. Abandoning my car didn't strike me as a good option.

But who was this and how long was I going to be trapped here? What if the guy got out to answer the call of nature? Why would they park out here? The answer to that seemed obvious. They were the security. What better place to watch who came in and went out? If the deal started to go bad back at Jimmy's, he could quickly pull out and block anyone from leaving. If I wasn't such a dumbass, I would have thought of that ahead of time and been prepared for the very guy that I was looking for to park in the very spot that I'd singled out as the best place to maintain a lookout.

I had to get a grip on myself. Beating myself up over bad planning wasn't going to help. The good news was that the deal must have been going down pretty soon since the home team had already taken the field. And the sooner this was over with, the sooner I could go someplace warm. I didn't have to remind myself that I was there for a reason, but being trapped had altered my priorities a bit. And, unfortunately, when the car came in I was so startled trying to keep from being seen that I didn't get a look at the driver.

I was getting ready to move up behind the car to get a look at the tag when the driver's door opened. I hunkered down again. I saw the car move and heard it squeak a little as the driver leaned on the front. Since I was on the passenger side, I couldn't see exactly what he was doing. *Probably keeping a lookout like I was supposed to be doing,* I thought. The night was cold and still and very, very quiet. I didn't dare make a sound.

After a couple more minutes, another car pulled into the industrial park. This one must have been the seller's. It was a very high-end BMW and was followed by a black Escalade. Both cars had guys in the front and back seats. I counted at least six big guys. Time seemed to stand still. I couldn't see or hear my nemesis, but I knew that he was only about ten feet away on the other side of his car. If he decided to take a walk, there was a good chance he'd either find my car or trip over me. What the hell had I been thinking?

The cold and lack of movement had left me with no feeling in my lower legs. If I had to run, I wouldn't be able to. I moved my hand back to my Glock, careful not to accidently turn on the flashlight that was attached to it. If things broke bad, I at least wanted to be able to defend myself. I tried flexing my leg muscles—nothing. It would have to wait until I could shift my position and get blood flowing again.

Thinking about my reason for being out there, I looked hard at the back of the car. Was there anything I could see that might give me a clue to whose car it was? But it was so dark. I could tell that the car was a newer model Toyota and dark colored, maybe burgundy. I looked at the hubcaps. I could see some detail in them because they were chrome and picked up some of the ambient light. Yes, those I could remember. And they might help guide me to the right year and make. Great. How many Toyota sedans are sold in America each year? But, of course, if Eddie was right and this was their security, and if their security was a bought cop, then all I'd have to do was compare it to local officers' cars. Would I be able to swear whose car it was? No. But it would set me on the right track.

Suddenly the BMW and the Escalade drove quickly out of the industrial park, so fast that the Escalade bottomed out with a scrape and a shower of sparks when it turned onto the main road. Ten minutes later the buyers drove out. I thought it odd that the man standing ten feet away waited five more minutes before getting into his car and following them. When he did get in the car and start the engine, I rolled over quickly and grabbed for my camera, hoping to get a photo of his tag. But the car sped off too fast.

I waited another couple of minutes, then tried to stand up. It wasn't happening. I had to roll onto my back, flexing my legs until the blood returned, bringing with it pins and needles that ran up and down my legs, leaving me close to tears.

During the trip home I had time to consider whether I'd wasted a golden opportunity to catch a bad cop.

CHAPTER EIGHT

I crawled out of bed at ten on Sunday and found a text message from Dad asking me to join him at a church brunch at Bethel First Christian Church on the south side. I texted him back and told him I'd meet him there. These meet-and-greets were part of his outreach to the black community. He was sincere in his desire to be the sheriff for everyone in Adams County.

My phone rang as I was pouring milk on my cereal.

"Hi, Eddie," I said in my *not thrilled you called* voice.

"How'd it go?"

"They showed up. I guess it went down. That's not a great place for one guy to surveil. Let's say I've had better nights."

"But my intel was good, right?"

"Seemed like it. Okay, honestly, your information did pan out and last night's failure was more about my execution. Happy?"

"Nooo. I'm not happy if you aren't happy." He actually sounded sincere.

"Look, Eddie, you did good. But these kinds of things are hard to pull off. I appreciate it. Really, I might have learned something from last night." I was thinking about the car and the tires. Could I turn that into useable information? I doubted it. "If I can develop it into something, I'll let you know. Meantime, keep your ear to the ground."

"Yeah, okay. Better luck next time, I guess."

"Thanks, Eddie, say goodbye now," I said and hung up on him. When I looked over at my breakfast, Ivy was happily drinking the milk out of my cereal. I wanted to scold her, but she looked so happy I just poured a little milk in another bowl for her. That earned me a purr, which brightened my mood a little.

When I pulled up to the church there were a few dozen cars in the dirt-and-grass parking lot and lots of men in suits and women dressed in their Sunday best. Little girls in fancy dresses and boys dressed like their fathers ran in and out among the adults. The church was a small, white-washed building with a rough hewn cross above the double doors that led into the sanctuary. Tables, already laden with food, had been set up on the lee side of the building in the sun. Groups of metal chairs and mismatched tables sat under the live oak trees scattered around the church.

I groaned when I saw Dad's van. That could only mean one thing—he'd brought Mauser. In the two years since Dad brought him home as a thirty-pound, nine-week-old puppy, Mauser had become as well known in Adams County as Dad. Meanwhile I lived in the shadow of both of them. I'd even been referred to as Mauser's brother a couple times, which was just dispiriting.

I heard laughter and, sure enough, half a dozen people were gathered around Dad and Mauser, chuckling as a boy of about ten got his first up close and personal encounter with the horse-dog. Mauser waited until the boy was close enough to touch him and then let out a friendly bark that shook the ground. The boy almost fell over backward, scrambling to hide behind his father to the amusement of everyone watching.

Then I saw my dad at his best as he knelt down beside Mauser and encouraged the boy to come forward and meet the dog. Slowly the boy came back and Dad showed him how to pet Mauser, who was eating up all the attention. Soon the boy was asking Dad if he could hold Mauser's leash and he dragged both Dad—still holding on to one end of the leash—and Mauser over to meet everyone else in his family.

On my way to catch up with Dad, I saw Marcus, Shantel's partner in the crime scene unit.

"Hey, Marcus."

"Larry, I was wondering if your dad brought you along to be part of the circus." Marcus smiled. He was dressed in a sharp pin-striped suit, making me feel underdressed in my corduroy coat and Dockers. Coming up behind Marcus was his wife, Esther, in a dark blue dress and matching hat.

"Honey, I hope you aren't here to drag him off to one of your nasty murders," she said, laughing loud enough for everyone there to hear.

"No murders today if I can help it," I said.

"Thank the Lord for small favors."

"Ignore her," Marcus said genially.

She hit him on the arm. "You better watch what you say." A young boy of about seven came running over and latched onto her leg, half hiding behind her dress. "Lord, here comes little trouble," she said. The boy looked like a one-quarter-sized version of his father.

"Nathan, right?" I asked, leaning over and talking to the boy. He nodded, but wouldn't come out from behind his mother.

"Dog!" the boy yelled and I looked up to see Dad and Mauser coming over to us. The boy was pointing, but keeping his mother between him and Mauser.

"Marcus!" Dad shouted, trying to control Mauser, whose excitement was reaching volcanic proportions. I stepped between the dog and Esther just in time to take the brunt of Mauser's greeting.

"Sheriff," Marcus said, shaking Dad's hand.

We talked Nathan into petting Mauser before Dad handed the beast over to me and went to talk with the women he called the Queens. They were a group of elderly women who were respected for their knowledge and contributions to the community. Dad had formed a relationship with them going back to the days when he was driving a patrol car and answering calls for service. He'd told me that they had helped him to learn more of what it meant to be a deputy in the rural black community than anyone else in law enforcement.

The Queens gathered around him, all talking at once. They liked him because he listened to them and, when he could, he acted on their complaints and suggestions. Dad had a different crime fighting philosophy than most police chiefs and sheriffs. He couldn't really care less about crime statistics. For him it was about preventing crime in his county, period. When he got a call about a drug house in a community, he made it go away. Some sheriffs would let their drug enforcement squads sit on a drug den for weeks or even months, making arrests and trying to move up the food chain to get the bigger dealers. But Dad would raid the house and sit on it until all of the druggies went somewhere else to do their business. If necessary, he'd park a patrol car in front of the house 24/7 until the word got out that the neighborhood was off limits.

So, when there was a problem, the Queens called Dad because they knew he'd take care of it. They trusted him and he trusted them. Most of them had his personal cell phone number. The county still had some dangerous neighborhoods and plenty of drugs, but not as much as most rural counties and the people in Adams County felt empowered by the sheriff's office, not threatened by it. Dad always said people just want safe neighborhoods to raise their kids. His job wasn't to save the world, just to save Adams County.

This morning I was trying to safeguard the lives of the kids and adults who came over to admire Mauser and to pose for photo-ops with the big ham. Keeping him from jumping on or whapping one of the kids with his tail demanded my full attention. If Dad spent half the time training Mauser as he did spoiling the big oaf, it would have been much easier. Of course I also had to answer all of the standard Great Dane questions: *Do you have a saddle for him? How much does he eat? How much does he weigh?* When you walk a Great Dane around, you get used to peoples' curiosity.

I watched Dad and felt guilty about all the secrets I was keeping from him. Not telling him about Henry was bad enough, but last night's expedition was pushing things further than I was comfortable with. If something went wrong, it was Dad who would get the blame and the bad publicity. But I couldn't predict how he would react to either situation. I was still determined to protect Cara's father because I believed him to be innocent. As for Eddie's warning about a bad deputy, knowing Dad there was a good chance he would overreact to the news that there was a possible mole in the department. Loyalty and integrity were two of the values he demanded from his deputies, and over the years very few officers had ever broken his trust. But he had a temper and a tendency to shoot from the hip. Shooting from the hip is fast, but not very accurate. No, I couldn't tell him yet. I'd try and get at least a little more information before dropping this bomb in his lap.

After a meal of fried chicken, greens and sweet potato pie, I helped Dad load Mauser back into his van and headed home. I called Cara on the way.

"I really need them out of my house, please," she pleaded. "Mom and Dad don't bother me at all when they're a hundred and fifty miles away. But being cooped up with them inside my little duplex is pushing me over the edge."

"Just hold on until Tuesday. I've got a few more things to check out. We know that—" I almost said Tyler and that's when I realized just how many secrets I was keeping these days. I hated being sneaky because I've never been good at it. "Timberlane bought the phone. It doesn't help, but at least we know. And I should have most of the preliminary reports back tomorrow."

"Okay." She tried to sound upbeat, but was failing miserably.

"I know this isn't necessarily the right time, but would you like to go out and get a bite to eat?" I was stuffed from the church picnic, but I wanted to see her and it would be a chance for her to get out of the house.

"Yes!" she said enthusiastically. "I'd go out with the devil himself to get out of the house."

"Ouch, that's not very flattering."

"Kidding, you know what I mean. When?"

A thought occurred to me. "Umm, make it five o'clock?"

"Sure. Perfect. Thanks."

I had decided that there was a little more digging I could do before I picked up Cara. I headed back out to Tyler's place. Pulling into the driveway, I looked over and saw what I was hoping to find. The old man was sitting on his porch.

I got out and headed his way. "Mr. Wright," I yelled, waving. I couldn't tell if I'd startled him awake or not.

"Hey, Mr. Deputy. What you doin' working on a Sunday? It is Sunday, isn't it?" he said with a smile.

"It's Sunday. I just wanted to ask you a few more questions, if you don't mind?"

"Come on in," he said as I got to the porch. As I climbed the stairs and opened the rickety old screen door, he laughed. "You know, it wouldn't break my heart if you brought an old man a beer when you come for a chat."

"I'll remember that next time," I said sincerely. "You mind?" I indicated an old lawn chair.

"Help yourself."

"You been doing okay?"

"Yeah. Cold weather's a bitch with my arthritis, but who's complaining."

"Last time I was here, I asked about anyone Timberlane had trouble with and you told me about the big man with the ponytail." He nodded. "What I didn't ask was, did you see anyone else around his trailer the last couple of days before he was killed, especially that afternoon and evening?"

I hated to admit that I hadn't done a very good job questioning him the last time we had a sit-down, but the truth was I got so focused on the man that Tyler had an argument with that I didn't dig any deeper.

"Well, not precisely," the old man said, screwing his face up in thought.

"How's that?"

"Well, I didn't see anyone go up to his house. But I think someone was looking at it."

"Who?"

"Someone in a car. Drove by and slowed down in front of my house and was going real slow past Timberlane's place."

"When?"

"Ahh, not too long after ponytail left."

"What'd he look like?"

"That's the problem. He was going that-a-way." Mr. Wright was pointing left to right. "So that he was on the other side of the car. I couldn't get a good look at his face. I couldn't tell much at all about him. He had on one of those hoodies. I was interested 'cause he slowed down as he came up to my driveway and I wondered if it was someone coming to see me. Not that I get that many visitors."

"What kind of a car was it?"

"Plain Jane. Nothing fancy. Not too old, not too new. It was dark, maybe dark green. American, I think. Ford possibly. Like I said, though, nothing that would make you remember it."

Great. Somebody possibly drove by in a generic car and looked at the murdered man's house on the day before the murder. That gave me a little less than nothing to go on.

"Is there anything else you can remember from that day or night?"

"I think I heard him go out. But that was late, after I'd gone to bed."

I stood up. "Thanks, Mr. Wright, you've been a big help," I lied. I shook his hand and, when I saw the tattered old Christmas wreath on his door, I vowed to come and sit and have a beer with him during the holidays.

CHAPTER NINE

When I pulled up to Cara's duplex she practically ran out to my car. I didn't even have time to get out before she dropped into the passenger seat.

"Drive," she commanded. "I love them, I really do, but I can't live with them. Not in my little house."

"Where do you want to go?" I asked as I backed out of her driveway.

"You know where I want to go?"

"Ah, no, that's why I asked," I kidded her.

"Buster's for an ice cream. Mom's been pushing soy this, tofu that and gluten-free whatever at me for days. I just want a big, gooey ice cream sundae," she said, relishing the sound of it.

"Sounds perfect to me." And it did. Even with the cold air, some frozen comfort food would be nice.

We rode in silence for a while before she turned to me. "I really do appreciate everything you're doing for me. I think I treated you a little unfairly before."

"I don't know. That whole situation was pretty weird, and it was only our second date. Good God, I even stuck you with the bill," I laughed and she smiled.

The sun was going down as I pulled up to Buster's Ice

Cream Stand, which had big old-fashioned Christmas tree lights strung through the live oak trees. We both got sundaes that overflowed with fudge, whipped cream and sprinkles and sat down at one of the picnic tables scattered around under the lighted oak trees.

For a few minutes we tackled our sugar- and fat-laden treats in silence. But watching Cara happily savor her ice cream, I felt like I had to pour out a little bit more of my heart to her.

"I shouldn't spoil the moment, but in the car it sounded like you might give us another chance." Having thrown it out into the open, I literally found myself holding my breath.

"I think so, yes." She was staring into her sundae as though she was reading the chocolate sprinkles and whipped cream swirls like tea leaves. "What I said is still true. I'm a little uncomfortable with you being a deputy. But I don't want to hide from the world. My mother has spent most of her life living in a world that she and Dad created. That's fine for them, but it's not what I'm looking for. I don't want to pretend that the world is a better place than it is. The world needs help. One of the reasons I work at the veterinary clinic is to help animals and people." She looked up into my eyes. "I see that same desire in you. And if by being a deputy you can make the world a little safer, then I think it's a good thing. What I couldn't stand is to watch it make you a harder, colder person inside. Of course, maybe I've just got a false impression of cops."

"No, it's hard to see the worst of people day in and day out. A lot of people can't handle it. But it can happen to other professions too. Teachers can become callous and burned out over time."

"The other problem is having someone I care about be at risk every day." She placed her hand on mine as she said those last words.

"I promise, I'll take good care of myself." I leaned in and kissed her lightly, coming away with whipped cream on my lips. We both chuckled when I licked it off. "I think you should always have your lips covered in whipped cream when we kiss."

She took a little bit of whipped cream on her spoon and gently flicked it at me.

"Don't start," I laughed, filling my spoon with fudge and cream and pretending I was going to send it flying at her. She raised her arms in surrender, so I stuffed the spoon in my mouth. We finished our sundaes while exchanging stupid smiles, then walked back to my car hand in hand.

We sat in the car for a while in front of her house. After a couple passionate kisses, she broke away. "I guess I can't sit out here all night."

"I'm not rushing you off." I was somewhere between mellow and ecstatic, if there is such a place.

"Buddy, you have to go to work tomorrow, check your reports and give my father the okay to go back home."

"You're right. I'll call you tomorrow afternoon."

She got out of the car. "I'll be at work, but don't hesitate to call my cell phone." She paused for a moment. "When everything is cleared up with Dad, I'm looking forward to spending time together."

"You're stealing my lines," I told her. She smiled, turned and waved over her shoulder as I watched her get safely into her house.

When I got to the office Monday morning, I still didn't have anything from forensics in my inbox. I had to call and poke the lab to get them to email me their preliminary findings. Toxicology showed exactly what you would expect. Blood alcohol level of .04, well below intoxication levels. Trace amounts of TCH, which translated to some pot smoked a few days earlier. Nothing that could have been used to knock him out.

Next I tackled the autopsy report. I opened it and then did what I usually did with Dr. Darzi's reports: called him for the verbal CliffsNotes edition.

"Pretty much what I told you the first day. He was repeatedly hung by the rope that was around his neck when he was found."

"And that would be consistent with him standing on a stool and having someone pull it out from under him and then replacing the stool several times?" I asked, remembering the indentations I had found under the tree branch.

"Yes, I said so originally and nothing discovered during the autopsy contradicted that."

"No bruising or lumps on the head, that sort of thing?"

"The only bruising was around the neck and consistent with the scenario you just described."

So he hadn't gotten into a fight with his killer, which meant they must have had a gun or knife in order to make him climb up on the stool with a noose over his head. He would have had to believe that the killer could and would shoot him, but he must've thought the murderer might release him if he didn't try to run. Interesting. Maybe it was someone he knew and trusted. Or at least someone he thought he knew. Unfortunately, this description still fit Henry.

I thanked Dr. Darzi and hung up. I didn't have anything that would exonerate Cara's father, but thinking about the gun gave me an idea. There weren't any houses close enough to the road or the hanging site for the residents to have seen anything, so we'd only done a cursory canvassing of the neighborhood. We hadn't expected anyone to see anything and no one had. But we hadn't bothered to ask about gunshots because there wasn't any indication that a gun was used. And the funny thing about eyewitnesses is that you usually have to ask specific questions to get decent answers. Asking *Did anything unusual happen last night?* wasn't nearly as good as asking *Did you see anyone or hear a gunshot?*

Pete came in just as I had this revelation, so I asked him if he was up for doing some door-to-door.

"Hell yeah," he said, looking at the pile of paper on his

desk.

It took us about an hour to find someone who thought he'd heard a sound around five that morning, but he couldn't decide if it was a gunshot or a car backfiring. The witness worked the early shift at the prison in the next county over, so he had to be up before dawn and was fairly familiar with what a gunshot would sound like.

"Yeah, I thought it could be a gunshot, but that's a weird hour to hear one. 'Course, if someone gets up and the raccoons are raiding his trash cans…" He shrugged. "I heard it clear, but it was pretty far away in that direction." He pointed in the general direction of the crime scene.

"We were lucky he was home," I said to Pete.

"It's getting close to the holidays so people take more time off."

"Want to push our luck?" I asked. He looked over at me and raised his eyebrows. "We could go look around and see if we can find where the bullet went."

"If there *was* a bullet, the odds of us finding it are…" He pretended to calculate. "Four trillion, one hundred ninety-five billion, eight hundred fifty-five million to one."

"Yeah, don't be a wet blanket."

But Pete was right. We walked around looking at trees and imagining possible lines of sight for about an hour before we admitted that we weren't *that* lucky.

On the way back to the office, my mind was going round and round about letting Henry go back to Gainesville. I knew I was letting my heart have too big of a say, but what little bit of law enforcement intuition I'd developed told me that he didn't kill Tyler. We did have one bit of evidence that spoke to his innocence. If the witness really did hear that gunshot, and if our murderer fired it, then it happened around five, before Henry left Cara's duplex. I made up my mind.

I parked in my favorite spot at the office and let Pete go

inside ahead of me. Then I called Cara. "Tell your dad he can go back to Gainesville, but nowhere else." *Let the crap fly,* I thought. *If I'm screwing up, I'm screwing up for a good cause.*

I climbed out of the car and was passing the second row of parked cars when something caught my eye. It took me just a minute to realize what I was looking at. It was a dark burgundy Toyota sedan. I stopped and looked around to see if anyone else was in the parking lot. A couple deputies were cutting the fool near the building, but they weren't paying any attention to me. I leaned over and took a good look at the tires. I closed my eyes and thought about those hubcaps that I'd spent the better part of an hour staring at. I opened my eyes. This could've been the car. No guarantees, even if it was the same make, model and color, since Toyota would have sold tens of thousands of them. But what were the odds?

I walked up beside the car and tried to nonchalantly look through the windows. There was a notebook and a blue light, the kind that you stick on the dash and plug into the auxiliary outlet. This was definitely a deputy's personal car. But which deputy?

I took out my phone like I'd just gotten a call. Talking out loud to an imaginary caller, I activated the camera and, as discreetly as possible, took a picture of the car's tag. I could have just memorized it, but I was already thinking of the file full of evidence that I might have to put together.

I could run the tag, but that would open me up to questions later. You can't run tags for personal reasons and, right now, I didn't have a case to tie this to, or even a good reason for running it. I could just wait until I saw who got into it, but I really wanted to know sooner rather than later. I could ask around, but then whoever's car it was would probably find out. That's when one of those little light bulbs went off over my head. I had to come up with a reason to go in and say, "Hey, someone's Toyota is something or other." A flat tire might be too over the top. I looked around again and bumped it pretty hard. Nothing. So it didn't have a sensitive alarm system.

Back to the tire. I looked around to make sure no one was watching, knelt down, unscrewed the valve cover and started letting air out. I just had to let out enough that it was noticeable. I didn't want to do anything too bad as this might not have even been the car I'd seen the other night. Finished, I stood up and looked. It was definitely low enough that anyone might notice it.

I went into the office and told the front desk sergeant that a burgundy Toyota in the parking lot had a tire that looked pretty low. He got on the intercom and announced the information to the office.

I casually went into a conference room on the back side of the building. I knew it had a window that faced out onto the parking lot. I watched. Ten minutes clicked by and I was beginning to think that the person was going to wait until they were ready to leave before checking on their car. And then I saw him, walking determinedly out to his Toyota. When I saw him and the car together, I finally remembered that I'd seen him driving it. It was Matt.

It didn't make sense. Matt was the last person I would have thought would be tied up with a drug gang. And I wasn't just thinking that because he was a nose-to-the-grindstone kind of deputy, but for practical reasons. He didn't have a wife or kids that were costing him money. It was laughable to think of him gambling his money away. I had never seen him take a drink. He'd never had any chronic pain, like the type that might get you hooked on painkillers. I knew that he'd put in applications to both the FBI and the DEA and had gotten as far as the interviews, which meant that he'd undergone very extensive background checks that would have revealed any financial difficulties or bad habits, like spending a fortune on prostitutes.

No, it just doesn't make sense, I thought as I watched him frown at the tire for a minute and then get in and drive off slowly. No doubt he was driving it across the street to the filling station to put air in it. Now that I thought about it,

Matt had been a lot nicer to me the last month. I assumed it was because of my hostage ordeal and solving the Kemper case, but maybe not. Could he have been trying to curb his acerbic personality so that he would fly a bit more under the radar? I was going to have to mull this over. *And keep an eye on Matt,* I thought. *How the hell am I going to manage that?*

CHAPTER TEN

I spent the next two days working on the half dozen cases that I'd been neglecting while working on the Tyler murder. On call Tuesday night, I had to disturb Ivy's sleep when I was called out for a burglary of the lowest type. Someone had broken into the First Methodist Church and stolen a pile of toys that was being stored for a Christmas charity. Normally a burglary doesn't warrant an investigator on the scene in the middle of the night and Deputy Edwards apologized for calling.

"I'm sorry, Larry, but jeez, what kind of Scrooge would steal toys for kids at Christmas? We've got to catch this guy."

"I'm with you," I said with all sincerity.

We didn't wake up the crime scene techs, but Edwards and I did a very thorough job collecting fingerprints and photographing the scene. We even found a shoeprint and some tire tracks where the idiots had run off the driveway. I knew Dad would want to do a personal Crime Stoppers PSA on this one.

My phone rang early on Thursday morning. I hunted for it, irritated because I figured it was Dad reminding me that I had to pick up Mauser, but then I realized that it wasn't his distinctive gunfire ringtone. I looked at the caller ID and a chill went down my back. It was Cara.

"Something's happened." Her voice was high and tense.

"Take a deep breath and tell me," I said, trying to wake up.

"Dad… There's been another murder," she said, and now my heart was racing.

"Where?" I stood up and headed for the kitchen to get a pen and paper.

"Gainesville. And…" She didn't seem able to get the words out.

"Tell me."

"Dad's been arrested. Please, can you go down and see what's going on?" I was already trying to think of anybody I knew who worked for law enforcement in Alachua County.

"Of course."

"I'm already headed that way." What had we ever done before we had cell phones?

"Listen to me, be careful. Keep your mind on your driving." Every year people are killed driving to help someone who's in trouble.

"I'm okay. But I think I really need you. Dad was confused and angry. He wasn't making a lot of sense and I'm afraid they won't listen to him."

"Don't worry. I'll be there," I said, not knowing if I'd be able to do anything. Departments can be pretty hostile to outside officers coming in and sticking their noses into another department's jurisdiction. Dad would probably know someone down there who could help, but that meant I was going to have to tell him everything.

"I'm getting my things together now. I'll call you when I have an ETA."

"Thank you. Thank you."

"Just drive safe."

I got cleaned up and put out the automatic feeder and waterer for Ivy. Depending on how long I was gone, I could call on a neighbor to look in on her. Next I packed a bag for a couple of nights. Done with my prep, I started to call Dad, then remembered about Mauser. Damn. I got in the car, deciding the best way to deal with it was to talk to Dad in person.

I was greeted by Mauser, bounding over and bumping into me as though he knew we were supposed to be roommates for the next few days. Hell, he probably did know since I could see the two suitcases Dad had packed for him.

Dad came out of the back when he heard Mauser bouncing around. "You're here early. Good."

"Dad, I've got something I need to talk to you about."

"Fine, as long as it doesn't involve you trying to get out of watching Mauser."

"Actually—" I barely managed to get the word out before Dad's face flushed. It was like watching the clock on a bomb counting down *3, 2, 1*. "Okay, no, wait," I said. "Listen to me first. Please."

Dad looked me hard in the eyes at the word "please." It isn't a word that either one of us uses with the other much. "Okay. Talk."

I explained about Henry. I had to go into a little more depth about my relationship with Cara than I wanted to, but I knew I didn't have much choice.

"You just let him go back home?" Dad yelled.

"All I had was circumstantial evidence against him. And my hunch says he didn't do it."

"That's not your hunch talking," he said, giving me the eye. Then he held up a hand. "Enough. Okay. What's done is done. I'll leave it up to Lt. Johnson as to whether you should be called on the carpet for this. You do remember that you have a supervisor?"

"Yes, sir," I said meekly.

"Good." He was sounding calmer. I hoped we weren't just in the eye of the hurricane. "Now, what's not negotiable is you taking care of Mauser for the next four days."

I started to open my mouth and protest, but the hand went up again. "But I'll make a deal with you. You can go down to Gainesville. You just have to take Mauser with you. You can take his van."

How gracious of you, letting me take the ratty dog van, I wanted to say, but I held my tongue. Getting to Gainesville and helping Cara was the important thing.

"Okay. Can you use your contacts in Alachua County to get me a liaison position on the investigation?"

He got real quiet. "Listen, we kid around and give each other a hard time. That's all part of the father/son thing we've got going, but I want you to sit down for a minute." He indicated the couch. Dad seldom let his good old boy mask slip and I wondered what was coming.

He sat in a chair across from me. Mauser, glad that the yelling was over, came and put his head on Dad's leg. Dad scratched the dog's ears as he talked. "When your heart gets tangled up in something this serious, you have to stop and step way back. Hardest thing you'll ever have to do is look into yourself and evaluate your motives when your heart is telling you one thing and the facts are telling you another. I don't want to help you get involved in something that's going to either ruin your career or break your heart. Or both."

I took a deep breath before I answered. "I know what you're saying. And I know you're trying to protect me, but I'm seeing this clearly. Strangely, when I'm with Cara, I see things clearer than I ever have."

"Love can bring clarity or confusion. Your mother brought clarity to my life, but I've seen many men and women that love delivered nothing to but bewilderment and conflict."

He looked at me hard, trying to evaluate… what? My maturity? My skills? Finally he said, "Enough. I trust you. I know you'll do the best you can. I'll talk to a couple people down there that owe me favors. Should be enough to get your foot in the door. Up to you if it gets broken."

"Guess we're going on a road trip," I told Mauser, who left Dad and came over to give me a single lick across my face with his giant slug of a tongue.

Once we were on the road to Gainesville, I called Cara. "I'm on my way," I reassured her.

"I don't know what to do." She was choking back tears. "A deputy told me they're holding Dad at the sheriff's office until the investigators are done at the crime scene. But they couldn't tell me how much longer it would be, or when they might release him."

"Just stay calm. We'll get it all sorted when I get there." I decided that I needed to lower her expectations concerning what I would and wouldn't be able to do. "We might not be able to get your dad out right away. It might even be a day or two before we can see him. Have you called a lawyer?"

"The co-op has a lawyer. Dad and he are great friends. He's trying to get in to see him, but according to the deputies, Dad hasn't asked to see a lawyer yet. If I know Dad, he's just clammed up. That's what he does when he's under too much stress. He just shuts down."

"Just hold on. I'll be there in about three hours."

After I rang off, I caught sight of a big, black blockhead in my peripheral vision. "I hope you're happy," I said, half turning to see Mauser's slobbering jowls sticking between the seats. He just looked at me and I passed a treat back to him.

"We need to have an understanding about this. It may be a vacation for you, but I have work to do." He heard me, but I doubt he was paying attention.

Halfway to Gainesville, Dad called.

"I've got you an in with Lt. Chavez. He's overseeing the crime scene."

"A lieutenant?"

"The murder took place at a state park, so it already has some jurisdictional issues."

Great, I thought. *More complications.* "Which park?"

"Devil's Millhopper on the north side of town. We went there once." The "we" was a loaded word since it included my late mother.

"I kinda remember."

"You were nine, maybe ten. Anyway, you should get there before they're done processing the crime scene."

"And you cleared it with Chavez?"

"No problem. I was one of his instructors when he went through the academy about a million years ago." I remembered Dad teaching classes at night for a dozen years when I was growing up.

"He had some issues I helped him work through. I told him his case is connected to one of ours and that I was sending you down there to assist. He actually sounded grateful."

I wondered how grateful Chavez would be if he knew I was trying to protect his chief suspect.

CHAPTER ELEVEN

It was just after two o'clock when I pulled into the park. I harnessed Mauser up for a quick walk before I went to find Lt. Chavez. Walking Mauser, I endured a few jibes from the deputies and park rangers, including: *We use bloodhounds, not horses down here*; and *Couldn't your mounted posse afford full-size horses?* The van plastered with "Ted Macklin for Sheriff" stickers had told them right away where I was from.

Another front had pushed through and the high temperature was going to be in the low fifties. I put the big guy back into the van with the windows down. He seemed perfectly happy to settle down for a nap after I fed him lunch.

The Devil's Milhopper is a sinkhole, one hundred and seventeen feet deep with a staircase zigzagging back and forth to the bottom. It looks like something out of the Mesozoic Era, with mosses and ferns growing on the sides as water trickles down from underground springs that were exposed when the hole formed hundreds of years ago. I found a group of deputies and crime scene techs about a quarter of the way down the stairs. A man who appeared to be in his mid-forties, with a rigid posture, dark skin and a thick black mustache, turned to me.

"Are you Deputy Macklin?" He stuck out a hand in a collegial manner. I took it and returned a manly shake.

"I am."

"I'm Lt. Carlos Chavez. Pleased to meet you. Your father is a great man," he said.

I decided it wasn't the time or place to present a counter-argument. "Thanks."

"He said you had a similar murder?"

"From what I understand."

"I'm a little puzzled how you learned about this one?" He had a fairly thick Latin accent and a disarming nature. Even though the question was asked lightly, I caught a sharp undercurrent to it. He clearly didn't like people leaking information.

Luckily, I'd thought someone might ask me this so I'd prepared the best answer I could come up with. "We've been in contact with Henry Laursen's family about our case. When I talked to them this morning, they told me that you were questioning him in connection with another murder." Pretty slick and all true.

"I think he is more than a suspect," Chavez said, smiling. "We found a body hanging off the rail." He pointed to obvious rope marks on the wooden railing facing in toward the sinkhole. I looked over the edge. It was about twelve feet down to a ledge. Someone on a four-foot rope would dangle a couple of feet off the ground.

"We've sent the body off already. Our techs just cut the rope off. Of course we've preserved the knot. Your victim was hanged?"

"Yes, from a tree."

"Comparisons between the rope and the knot should be interesting," he said and I had to agree.

"How did you find the suspect?"

"He was still in the parking lot. Our deputies got a tip that something weird was going on here. When one of our cars pulled into the park, the suspect ran to his truck and tried to get away. The deputy detained him by putting him in the back of his patrol car until he could figure out what was going on. Looking around, he found the body hanging off the rail."

"Did the suspect say why he tried to get away?" I probed.

"The usual: *Cops make me nervous, always trying to get people in trouble.* Never mentioned a murder up your way. No surprise. The best part, we found a piece of rope in the back of his truck that looks like it could be a match for the noose." Chavez was clearly feeling good about tagging Henry for this murder. *Not good*, I thought.

It was then that someone shouted down to us. "Hey, your horse is trying to get loose."

I turned to Chavez. "Long story. I'll be right back."

"Don't bother. A couple more pictures of the marks in the wood and we're done here. I'll walk up with you. What horse?"

"Probably best if you just see him," I said, hurrying up the steps. When I got to the parking lot I was met by the sight of Mauser with both front paws out the window and his back feet barely touching the inside of the van. He'd apparently thought he could jump out the window, but got stuck halfway. He looked up at me with an open-mouthed grin. After a little pushing and shoving, I got his front end back inside the van. Then I took him out on his leash and he bounded over to Chavez, who was laughing heartily.

"I remember. Yes, I remember coming over to your house. You were young. You all had a giant dog then."

"Yeah, he was much better trained than this monster," I said, trying to keep Mauser from jumping up on Chavez. "My mother made him toe the line. Come to think of it, she kept all of us on our toes."

"Oh, yes, I was sorry to hear about your mother. She was always very nice to me."

"Thank you," I said, wrestling Mauser back into the van.

Chavez's phone rang. "Yes?" He listened for a bit. "You've interviewed them? And you say he lived at the co-op? I see. No, let's not book him yet. I want to see if I can get him to confess." Chavez was smiling at me as he put his phone back in his pocket.

"I think we will be booking Mr. Laursen for murder very soon. That was one of my investigators. He's been interviewing people who live next door to our victim. Seems that our suspect is on the board at the co-op where the victim lived. Even better, my friend, they had a fight last night. Multiple witnesses. We'll see if Laursen will confess when I confront him with this news. We might be fighting over who gets to prosecute him first." He smiled from ear to ear. The smile was that of a cat who's trapped a mouse. I would not want Chavez on my trail.   "Would you like to sit in on the interview?"

I didn't want to do that because I couldn't predict how Henry might react if he saw me with Chavez. I thought it was possible that he might think I'd betrayed him. "If I could watch, that would be great. But I'm not sure what tack we might want to take when we go after him for our murder. Might be best not to have him associate me with this investigation."

"Smart," Chavez said. "You can follow me." He went over to an unmarked car and climbed in.

I called Cara on the way to the Alachua County Sheriff's Office. All I could do was prepare her for the possibility that her father was going to be charged with murder.

"I understand," she said, choking back her emotions.

"I'll come and see you as soon as I can." I realized I was on very slippery ground now. If I revealed anything from the interview, I could be charged with obstructing justice. And by not telling Chavez of my relationship with the family, I was violating his trust and jeopardizing my freedom. We were definitely in tangled-web territory.

After parking at the sheriff's office, I was debating what to do with Mauser when Chavez came over and told me to bring him in. *What the hell*, I figured. I led the big galoot into the building to the sound of much "oohing" and "aahing." Chavez had me terrorize a young deputy coming out of a bathroom. The poor guy let out a small scream as if he'd just seen a bear. I realized at that point that Mauser was a huge asset, emphasis on huge. People were focusing on him and not me, and I was also benefiting from the goodwill the big monster was generating.

Finally all the laughter died down and Chavez led me into a room with monitors where I could watch the interrogation. The knowledge that I was deceiving the deputies around me gave me pause. *Is this how Matt is feeling now? Is he working for the other side and constantly having to guard his secrets?* It was a chilling thought.

On the monitor I could see Henry sitting in a room that was small and furnished with only a metal table and a couple of uncomfortable-looking chairs. He had his head down on the table. My heart went out to him. He looked totally alone and abandoned. How many suspects had I seen like this that I thought they were getting what they deserved? If I didn't know Henry and didn't care for his daughter, would I think *he* was getting what he deserved? Maybe. The evidence against him was stacked high.

Henry looked up when Chavez entered the room carrying a folder. Was that hope in his eyes? Did he think everyone had come to their senses and he was going to get to go home?

"How are you holding up?" Chavez asked in a friendly way, pulling a chair close to Henry and sitting down.

"I'm okay. Can I go now?" From Henry's tone it was obvious he knew that he wasn't getting out yet.

"I've got just a few more questions before we let you go." Chavez opened the folder he was carrying.

"Sure, I'll tell you anything I can to help."

"Great. First, did you know the victim?" Chavez asked very matter-of-factly.

"Yes, I told the Adams County deputies all about that." I realized then that they hadn't told Henry exactly *why* they were holding him. This wasn't unusual. The lead investigator would want to see the suspect's reaction when he told him.

"No, Mr. Laursen, I'm talking about our victim. Did you know the person that was killed this morning?"

"What? What? Who?" Poor Henry was completely confused.

"Why do you think that we brought you in for questioning?"

"I... don't know. Maybe because I tried to run away from the officer at the park."

"Didn't he tell you why he was at the park?"

"He just said that there was a disturbance. There'd been a call about a problem. That's all I know." Henry's voice was rising and his hands were on the table, anxiously grappling with each other.

"A person was found in the sinkhole hanging off the rail, Mr. Laursen. And when an officer showed up, you tried to run."

Henry's mouth was hanging open in confusion and disbelief.

"Did you know the victim?" Chavez was good. He was avoiding using a masculine or feminine pronoun for the victim. If Henry let on that he knew it was a male, then Chavez could assume that he'd been lying about his ignorance that a murder had been committed at the park. Chavez was also doing a great job of keeping Henry off balance.

"I didn't even know there was a victim. Who was it?" There was fear in Henry's voice and in his eyes. I don't think it was an emotion he was used to.

"You're telling me that you didn't know that someone had been killed at the park?"

"I didn't. I swear I had no idea." He sounded completely honest to me. Was I just biased?

"Okay," the lieutenant said without judgment. I knew what was coming next as he shuffled through the papers in his folder. He pulled out a picture and slid it across to Henry.

"Here is a picture of the victim."

I couldn't quite make out the photo over the CCTV, but I knew it would be the most gruesome photo of the body that they had. Anything to shake, rattle and roll the suspect.

"Oh, God, oh, no, no." I thought Henry was going to fall off his chair. He grabbed his head with both hands as if to shut out the world and began to rock back and forth. It was painful to watch.

"Do you know him?" Chavez asked again, tapping the photo with his finger.

Henry had shut down. He continued to hold onto his head and rock in the chair. I could see Chavez watching him, trying to determine if Henry was acting, if he was upset because he was being confronted by his crime, or if Henry was legitimately just shocked and scared. I was confident it was the latter.

Chavez gave Henry some more time to compose himself, but finally he leaned forward again and said, "Mr. Laursen, I can see that you are upset, but I need you to answer my questions if you want to go home." Give the suspect hope that if he cooperates he can get what he wants: freedom. "You want to go home, right?"

I was trying to send Henry a telepathic message: *Ask for a lawyer and refuse to answer any more questions.* That would be Henry's best chance to go home now.

"I know him," Henry, failing to get my message, said in a very small voice.

"What is his name?"

"Tommy."

"Do you know his last name?" Chavez pushed.

Henry thought for a minute. "Gibson. That's it."

"How do you know him?"

"He lives at the co-op," Henry said mechanically. I knew that he wasn't even thinking about whether or not to answer the questions now. Chavez had turned his world upside down, and he would answer any question asked with the hope that it would be the last question before the doors magically opened and he walked out a free man.

"The co-op that you help to run?"

"Yes."

"What's your relationship with him?" Not accusatory. Not *Did you have a fight with him yesterday?* A good interrogation is all about letting the suspect dig his own grave. Let him lie and then let him know that you knew the truth all along. Mind games.

"I just… He just lived there. I knew him." It was painful watching Henry try to hide something. He was really, really bad at it.

Mauser put his head on my knee as though he knew I needed some comforting, or he was just unsettled because he wasn't the center of attention for five minutes. I patted his head absent-mindedly, focused on Chavez's next question.

"You were friends?" Chavez tried to lead him down a blind alley.

"Noooo. Not friends, exactly. I just rented him the trailer he was staying in. Not me exactly, it's the co-op's house. We have about a dozen we rent out."

"But you were on good terms?" Chavez's voice was completely neutral, but you could tell by Henry's body language that he had finally seen the trap that had been laid for him.

"Well, not recently." He looked down at the floor.

"You had been on good terms, but you weren't now. What changed?"

Henry didn't look up. He mumbled something.

"What?"

"I got a phone call."

Chavez didn't say anything. He just let the silence beg to be filled.

"I got a call that said that Tommy had done something… Something horrible."

CHAPTER TWELVE

For the first time, I saw that Chavez had been taken by surprise, but he recovered quickly. "Who called you?"

"I don't know. If I had my phone, I could show you the number," Henry said, but I got the feeling he was hiding something about that too.

"Did you recognize the voice?"

Henry hesitated a fraction of a second too long. "No."

"Henry, if you want to go home today, you can't lie to me. You recognized that voice, didn't you?" Chavez was in good-cop mode now.

"I didn't at the time. But I think I do now. It was the same person who got me to go to... to where Timberlane was hanged."

This was all news to Chavez, and he was probably wishing that he'd questioned me more about my case. But he didn't let his confusion show. "So someone, someone who you now think called you to the murder scene in Adams County, called you and told you that Gibson had done something. Done what?"

You could tell by the way Chavez had said it that he didn't believe it for a minute. In fact, he was probably wondering if Henry was delusional, or pretending to be.

Watching Henry's continued humiliation at the hands of Chavez, I knew that if my relationship with Cara continued and if we managed to pull her father out of this nightmare, I would never be able to let Henry know I had seen this interview.

Henry went on to answer Chavez's question. "He said that Tommy had attacked a woman and that he'd been in league with Timberlane." Henry stopped at the mention of Timberlane.

"Didn't you ask him who he was?"

"Yes, but he said that didn't matter and that I knew Timberlane and Gibson were monsters."

"Is that true? Were they monsters?" Chavez was asking Henry to give him his motive for killing them. I silently begged Henry to shut up.

"Yes. I know that now," Henry said in the dull, flat tone of a defeated man.

"You knew they were monsters so you had to do something?"

"Yes," Henry said and my heart leaped in my chest. Was he about to confess?

"What did you do, Henry? It's okay. If they were monsters, you had no choice."

"I kicked them out. When I caught Timberlane molesting that girl, I kicked him out. I wasn't going to pay him, but the board insisted that I give him his check so he'd go away and quit harassing everyone."

"And Gibson?"

"Him too. I should have done it right after I threw Timberlane out. They were always hanging out together. I should have known that he was probably involved in anything that Timberlane was, but I didn't. The caller, I knew he was telling the truth so I went straight to Gibson and told him he had to get out."

"How did he take it?"

"He was mad. Gibson was a hothead, just like Timberlane."

"He wouldn't go?"

"No, but I told him that if he wasn't out by the morning I'd come and…" Henry knew he'd walked into another trap.

"What did you tell him you'd do?"

"Kick his ass."

"You didn't say you'd kill him?"

"No! Just kick his ass."

"But you all argued?"

"I would call it that. He told me to go screw myself. He had a lease and wasn't going anywhere. I told him I'd give him the money for the rest of the month, but he said it was Christmas and he wasn't leaving until the New Year."

"Of course that made you angry."

"That's when I told him to be out by morning or I'd kick his ass."

"What did he say when you threatened him?"

From the look on Henry's face, it was clear he hadn't thought of it as a threat. "He said I was an old man and he'd beat the crap out of me if I tried it."

"It sounds like Gibson was a pretty nasty guy. What happened when you found out he hadn't moved out?"

"I didn't. I hadn't gone to check."

"You were all upset and demanded that he leave before morning, but come morning you didn't bother to check and see if he *had* left?" Chavez was turning up the heat a little bit.

"I've struggled with my anger in the past. I didn't want to get in another fight with him. I thought if I gave him some extra time before I checked on him…" Henry shrugged.

He'd already given Chavez more ammunition by telling him that he'd had anger management issues in the past. This interview was the perfect example of why lawyers tell everyone, no matter how innocent they are, to never voluntarily talk to the police. When a cop asks a question, the answer should always be *I want a lawyer*. Thinking about how close I was to actually obstructing justice, I wondered if *I* was going to have to call a lawyer. I needed to solve this as quickly as possible.

"Okay, let's go back to this morning. What did you do when you woke up? Take me through your day up to the time that you saw the deputy."

"It was cold so I got up to put some wood in the stove and got the fire going for Anna. She hates to get out of bed when it's cold. I did a few chores and then headed out to the Millhopper."

"You go to the Millhopper every day?"

"No, I go three times a week, usually. I go on Tuesday, Thursday and most Sundays."

"Why?"

"I go up and down the stairs ten times, exercise. A couple of years ago I was warned about my blood pressure. I like going up and down the Millhopper. If I try and walk around the co-op, I end up having to stop every couple of minutes to talk to people. The air there is a lot cleaner than walking along the roads or in town and, besides, it's only five minutes from my house." He shrugged. That explained a lot. If it was his routine, then other people would probably know about it.

"Do you go at the same time every day?" Chavez asked the right question.

"Tuesday and Thursday I'm almost always there around eight when they open the gate. The rangers will back me up. I know both of the regulars by name, and they know me. Sundays, it all depends on what's going on. If we have company or are going to have a special dinner or something like that, I go when I can or not at all." Just thinking about normal life was calming him down.

"When you got to the park today, what did you do?"

"Not much. I got out of the truck and started down the trail to the Millhopper."

"So you went and walked up and down the stairs?" Chavez was incredulous, wondering if Henry was going to claim that he didn't see the body.

"No. I never got there."

"Why not?"

"I got part way down the trail and thought about my cell

phone. So much has been going on that I thought I'd better keep it with me. I normally don't bother. I don't want to get a call about someone's plumbing or leaky roof or what have you. Walking through the park and up and down those stairs is *my* time. Really, that's why I've kept it up for a couple years. It's peaceful. But I thought I better have my phone today so I went back to get it out of my truck."

"That's when the deputy found you in the parking lot?"

"I'd just got back to the truck when he pulled in. I wasn't worried at first, but then he looked at me. I don't know. It was like I was nineteen again. I got spooked. He saw it. We were like a dog and a rabbit."

Chavez shuffled through the papers in the file folder again. He pulled out a picture and pushed it across the table to Henry. "Have you ever seen this before?"

Henry looked at it with a puzzled expression on his face. "It's a piece of rope."

"That's right. Have you ever seen this particular piece of rope before?"

"I don't know. It's just a piece of rope." I could see Henry putting two and two together. "I didn't hang anyone. Not the guy in Adams County or the one here. That's crazy."

"What would you say if I told you we found this piece of rope in the back of your truck?"

Henry looked trapped. He saw his hope of going home fading with each question. "I don't know. I don't think that piece of rope was in my truck, but I have a lot of stuff in it. It's my work truck. I spend half my day fixing things around the co-op. Sometimes I work with other people, and they get things out of my truck or put stuff in. There's wood and metal scraps back there and all kinds of trash. I should clean it out. I just don't."

"We're pretty sure that this piece of rope came from the same rope that was tied around the victim's neck. Now do you see our problem?" Chavez's acting skills weren't up to making this sound like he thought it was a problem.

"You think I killed them. I didn't. I don't know how I

can prove it to you."

"If you can't prove that you didn't kill them, and we have evidence that says you did…" Chavez gave a *what can I do* shrug.

"Let's, for the sake of argument, say you killed them." Henry started to protest, but Chavez held up a hand to stop him. "We're just hypothesizing right now. Okay. If you did it, but could give me a good reason *why* you killed them, then maybe we can help you. You said that they were monsters. Rapists? Molesters? If that's true, it's understandable that you wanted to kill them. Now I'm not actually talking about doing it. First, tell me, did you *want* to kill them?"

This is a classic technique to get a confession. Get the suspect to admit that he wanted to commit the crime and then work it around until he admits to having *done* the crime. Of course, using this method, you can also get innocent people to confess to horrible crimes that they didn't commit.

I watched for another forty-five minutes as Chavez took Henry to the edge of a confession over and over again. Each time I was afraid that Henry might just fold and give Chavez what he wanted. But Henry, even in his emotionally exhausted state, was strong. Each time he said no. Always no. Some interrogators would have kept badgering Henry until sleep depravation and exhaustion led the suspect to confess, whether they were guilty or not. I gained a margin of respect for Chavez when he got up and left the room. He came in and told me that he wasn't going to pressure Henry any further, but he felt that he had no choice but to book him for the murder.

"I'm pretty sure we can obtain more physical evidence. We found a knife in the back of the truck which might have been used to cut the rope. Forensics will take a while to make that final determination. But if they say it could have, and we have witnesses that have seen Laursen with the knife in the past, and it was found in his truck… I think the State Attorney will like that."

I was sick at heart. I had to do something for Cara. "I've

been in contact with his family. I think they might still be cooperative, even now that you've decided to press charges. But it would help if I could tell them that he's being booked and let them know what their options are for seeing him."

"Sure. That's fine," he said. Chavez was in a good mood. He had a probable suspect behind bars on a case that tread on state feet. He was petting Mauser and telling him what a good boy he was. I felt like nudging the dog and telling him not to fraternize with the enemy. Though, honestly, it was hard to see Chavez as an enemy. If I were in his shoes, I'd have been pushing things in the same direction that he was. On the other hand, if he knew about my relationship with Cara, I was fairly certain that he'd see *me* as the enemy.

"Do you know of a motel around here—" I started before he interrupted me, starting to list half a dozen and where they were located. "—that will take him too," I broke in, pointing to Mauser.

"Ha, ha, that's a little trickier. I'll call a couple up and see if I can get you two in someplace."

Twenty minutes later I was on my way to a motel on the outskirts of town that had said they took pets and didn't have a size limit. Chavez apparently knew the management and warned them that they might want to rethink their policy after they saw what he was sending them. I promised Chavez I would bring him up to speed on the Timberlane case the next time we got together.

I hit the speed dial for Cara's number. Maybe it was wishful thinking that had led me to add her number to my favorites. I explained the current situation with her father. Again I told her that the sooner they got him a lawyer, the better. Visiting hours were between two and five. I looked at my watch and it was already almost four.

"I'm sorry that I can't drive you to the jail. But if Chavez heard about it, he'd have some hard questions for me."

"I understand. I don't want to get you into trouble," she said.

"Tell your father that he has to ask for a lawyer and not

to answer any more questions until he's spoken to one. Also, tell him he needs a criminal lawyer, not some friend that does contract law or environmental law or something."

"I will. I know you're right. I just can't believe the mess we're in. And Mom is in complete denial."

"Maybe seeing your father through Plexiglas will wake her up. I won't lie to you. Someone has done a royally good job of framing him for these murders. It's going to take a lot of luck and hard work to get him out of jail."

She was quiet and I was afraid that I might have been too brutally honest. Finally she said, "I know you're right, and I appreciate you being honest about it. I don't want to be like Mom. If things are bad, I want to know how bad."

"That's the only way to be prepared for the fight. Call me after you've seen him."

CHAPTER THIRTEEN

I pulled up to the Alligator Motor Lodge. The motel looked like it had been built in the 1940s or '50s, but it appeared clean and well cared for. There were several one-story block buildings with half a dozen rooms each. The office was in the front of the complex. Its door was covered in a variety of stickers touting AAA, the MCA Motor Club and a few more organizations that I didn't think had existed for decades.

A thin woman in her sixties with wild, highly unnatural red hair and wearing enough jewelry to stock a small store was behind the desk, scrolling through something on her computer. She looked up and a huge smile spread across her face.

"Hello! May I help you?" She was positively beaming. She had a tag on her bright green blouse that read: *Mrs. Perkins, Manager/Owner.*

"Yes, Lt. Chavez with the—" I didn't have a chance to finish before she came running around the desk.

"Ohhhh, yes, you're the fellow with the Great Dane! Where is that big boy?" She started looking around as though she expected him to walk in on his own.

"He's out in the car. I need to let you know that he's still a bit of a puppy. He hasn't stayed in a motel before…" I hoped she'd understand what I was implying.

"Ohhh, the poor boy. Probably going to be a little nervous." She winked at me. "Worried he might damage something? Never you mind. I have the perfect room for those puppies that are a little more excitable." She grabbed a key from a rack in the back of the office. I didn't even know there were motels that still used keys. She pulled out a form for me to fill out and took my credit card. *Why didn't I think to grab Dad's credit card?* I thought, watching her zip mine through her machine. God knew how many charges Mauser would rack up.

Paperwork done, we went outside and I retrieved Mauser from the van. He immediately recognized a fan and ran over to Mrs. Perkins. Ten minutes later, after she'd made over him and I'd given her all of his statistics, we were on our way to the room. I thought it odd that we went past all the buildings out front to a smaller building in the far corner. Mrs. Perkins opened the door and the distinct odor of musty dog hit me. She entered and started opening the windows, which were small and set high on the walls. A queen bed with a saggy mattress took up the middle of the room. The room was furnished like a cheap motel from the 1980s. All of the furniture looked like a colony of beavers had tried to drag if off and the doors looked like someone had tried to keep a bobcat in the room.

"Yes, this is our bad boy room." She scratched Mauser's ears. "It's not your fault, is it?" She gave me a pointed look.

"My dad is pretty lenient with him."

"Yes, of course. There are towels in the bathroom. I'll tell Stella not to clean the room while you're here. You just let me know if you need anything. To-da-loo," she said, giving Mauser a couple more scratches before leaving and closing the door behind her.

"Great, we're in a cell together. This is all your fault. I told you, you need to grow up on your own. You can't count on Dad teaching you anything." He gave me a *whatever* look and hopped up on the bed.

I went back out and moved the van next to our Gulag-inspired room. After dragging all of Mauser's luggage into the room, I made his dinner.

"Okay, big guy, I'm going out to get myself something to eat. Are you going to be okay?" He rolled over on his side and closed his eyes. "Guess so."

I'd just finished dinner at a pizza joint when my phone went off. It was Cara, calling to report on her visit with her dad.

"Larry, it was awful seeing him like that. But I've convinced him to let me find a lawyer. A real lawyer."

"How's your mom doing?"

"She's okay, but she goes kind of blank every now and then."

"Would you mind if I came out there? I want you to show me around Timberlane's old trailer and where Gibson lived. I'll need the full fifty-cent tour."

"They went through Gibson's trailer today. It's all taped off."

"We'll figure it out," I assured her, then got directions to the co-op.

The Laursen home was an interesting amalgamation of styles. It looked like it had been built by a dozen different builders who never consulted each other. Inside it was cozy and eclectic, with large cushy furniture that had seen better days and that was covered in pillows and throws. The floor was a beautiful hardwood with hand-woven area rugs adding bright colors. The walls were covered with handmade arts and crafts. All of the hardware on the cabinets and furniture was intricate wrought iron.

"Dad forged all of the ironwork," Cara told me as I admired the hinges and door handles. "Mom made some of the art and the rest were gifts from friends around the world."

"How's your mother?"

"She took some herbal tea and had a bath before lying down." Cara went over to a door and opened it a little, listening at the crack. She closed the door softly. "She's sleeping."

"I know it's dark, but I'd still like to get a lay of the land."

"Of course. Come on." She grabbed a flashlight before opening the door and I followed her into the night.

It was cold out, and quiet. Even though we were just outside of the Gainesville city limits, only the occasional barking dog cut the night air. There were no sidewalks in the co-op and the roads were packed dirt. I'd passed only two houses coming in. One was a traditional ranch style and the other a small wooden A-frame. A few of the houses had Christmas lights on.

"This is the road you came in on. It branches right and left when it reaches Mom and Dad's house." We turned right out of their driveway. "In both directions there are two circles off of each road. Each of the four circles has about ten lots around it, and most of the lots have someone living on them. Plus there are a few houses, like Dad's, along the feeder roads." She sounded like a professional tour guide.

"You've done this before?"

"Sorry, showing people around was one of my jobs when I lived here." She sounded wistful. "You know, I miss it sometimes. The co-op is a real community. Forty families live here permanently, and then we've always had a couple dozen people who are here on their way to somewhere else. That was the case with both Timberlane and Gibson. Not that I knew either one of them. Both of them came here after I'd moved up to Calhoun."

"Did they live in the same house?"

"No, but their trailers were next door to each other. Dad said that Gibson was here first and Timberlane came about two months later. Dad wasn't sure if they knew each other before they met here or not. But they seemed chummy right off."

We came to the road leading to the first circle and Cara

switched off the flashlight. The moon was full and even with the light cloud cover, we were able to see the sandy road in the dark. It would have been very romantic if her father hadn't been in jail for murder. I reached out and touched her hand. She took mine and held it tight.

"That's Gibson's." She pointed to a singlewide trailer that had crime scene tape across the dirt driveway. Letting go of my hand, Cara turned on the flashlight again and led the way around the tape. More tape crisscrossed the trailer door.

"Do you know if the investigators took anything?"

"Cyril—he lives over there." She pointed the light to a small house with wood siding. A light was on in the front windows. "Cyril said that they took a couple boxes of stuff."

An old Ford sedan was parked up close to the trailer. "Shine the light in there." The interior had fast food effluvium scattered over the seats and the floorboards. The bags and cups weren't very old. "Is this Gibson's?"

"I guess. But I don't really know."

We walked around the trailer. At the back door, Cara produced the keys. I pulled some of the crime scene tape off and we went in. An odor of stale beer and old pot smoke permeated the air.

"You can turn the light on. Cyril isn't going to tell the deputies anything. He's one of Dad's oldest friends. When I told him that they were holding Dad, he wanted to get a gang together to go break him out."

The light was dim and showed a mess eerily similar to Tyler's place. They were certainly birds of a feather. A few drawers and cabinets were open. It was hard to tell what was the result of Gibson's bachelor lifestyle and what had been left a mess by the crime scene techs. I rummaged around the clutter. There weren't many personal items. A couple of suitcases worth of clothes, some car and gun magazines, boots and some tools.

"Is this the co-op's?" I asked, looking at a professional-quality tool box, tools and tool belt.

"I doubt it. Dad makes sure that the co-op's stuff goes

back in the shop."

"The shop?"

"That's what everyone calls it. The big metal building behind our house. That's where all the tools and supplies are kept. There's even a place where you can work on a car. A lot of the folks who stop here need some car repairs to get back on the road."

"Gibson worked around here too? Like Timberlane?" I still felt bad that I was hiding the fact we knew his name wasn't Timberlane, but that information could be useful when we found a suspect. And even though I refused to think of Cara's dad as a suspect, I couldn't just go around giving out information on the case.

"Dad said he did a little bit around here. Helped out Timberlane some, but he mostly got odd jobs doing construction work. Dad said Gibson liked doing... something... framing, that's it. Gibson liked to do the framing on houses."

I looked at the tools and they were mostly what you would expect from someone working with wood. Opening the toolbox, there was a professional-grade drill, nails, a hammer, screws, a large folding knife and a partially used roll of duct tape. The duct tape made me think of the Tyler/Timberlane murder. His hands had been bound by duct tape. Was it possible that Gibson murdered Tyler? That could make some sense. They knew each other well enough that Gibson could have had a motive.

Could the duct tape around Tyler's wrists have come from this roll? Mind you, there is a roll of duct tape in just about every house in America, and it's often used by the big three—rapists, murderers and kidnappers—so there was little reason to think that there was a connection between this roll and what was used in our murder. But I had to check. I couldn't take it now. I'd have to wait until I came back here with Chavez or one of his men. But I was definitely going to send it to our lab to compare it with the tape taken off of Tyler.

I didn't see anything else of interest in the house. Again my mind tried out the idea of Gibson as Tyler's murderer. Of course, that begged the question of who killed Gibson. The answer to that question was probably not the ghost of Tyler. It would require more thought and didn't solve the problem that we still needed a suspect to take Henry's place in jail.

"Is this a good time to talk to Cyril?" I asked as we walked away from Gibson's trailer.

"He'll be glad to talk to you if he knows that you're trying to get Dad out of jail."

As we headed toward Cyril's house my phone rang. It was Mrs. Perkins from the motel.

"Mauser is barking and whining," she said flatly.

"I'm really sorry, ma'am. I'll be done here shortly and I'll get back as soon as I can."

"He sounds very unhappy."

"I'm sorry."

"If you don't mind, I'll go in and check on him. I could read him a bedtime story." She said this in a completely serious voice.

"I guess. If you don't mind."

"Not at all. It's the poor boy's first night in a strange room. I'll see about him. You get back when you can."

"Okay, thanks." Mauser had that effect on people. They'd bend over backwards to make excuses for him and go out of their way to make life easy on him. *If I only had half his charm, my life would be a lot easier*, I thought.

CHAPTER FOURTEEN

Cyril Riggs looked like the world's oldest hippy. After Cara introduced me, Riggs invited us into his small house. He might have been a hippy, but from the looks of his house he was on the OCD spectrum. It was minimalist and clean. The few art pieces around the room were Oriental.

He pointed us to some cushions neatly arranged in the middle of the floor.

"We can stand."

"No, please," he insisted. I struggled to get to the ground and sit on the pillows with my legs crossed and watched as he seemed to magically lower himself to a lotus position. His shoulder-length hair and beard were grey with streaks of a darker color, a mere memory of his original hair. He smiled at us with a calm demeanor.

"I need to know everything you can tell me about the men who were killed, Timberlane and Gibson."

"They were bad news." He looked at Cara, "I'm sorry, but I told your father that they were both rotten. But he was always willing to give people a chance. I should have just kicked their asses and booted them down the highway."

He said this last so calmly that it took me a minute to register what he'd said. I took a better look at him. He was probably in his seventies, but his arms were toned and the muscles looked like they got regular workouts. *Be careful judging books*, I told myself.

"How did you know they were bad?" I asked him.

"Because I've been rotten myself. Or at least I spent too much time in my youth around people who were no good. You know, I met Charles Manson before the murders? I even went out to the Spahn Ranch a couple of times when the Manson family was there. Later I spent a couple years with some pretty ugly biker gangs. These guys were dangerous."

"Was there anything specific?" I asked.

"If they weren't ogling the women, the two of them always had their heads together plotting something. I tried to keep an eye on them. Figured they'd steal anything that wasn't tied down. Not that most of us keep anything that could easily be turned into cash. Mostly it was the way they treated women. I warned them once about Terri. She was collecting wood and stuff for her art projects and I caught them watching her. Told them to keep their eyes on something else."

"How'd they take that?"

"We'd already had a couple of run-ins. They tried to intimidate me. Gave me the squint eye."

"What happened?"

"Nothing. You can't intimidate someone who isn't afraid of you. Both of them were cowards at heart. I just had to make sure they didn't get the drop on me. I was glad when Henry finally read Timberlane the riot act and chased him off."

"You said they gave a woman named Terri a hard time?"

"I'm not sure if she noticed or not. I just caught them watching her. It was just a couple days after that that Henry sent Timberlane packing."

I turned to Cara. "I'd like to talk to Terri."

"She's in Europe taking some art classes or something. But her parents are here. They were in a car accident not too long ago and are staying here while her father's been in and out of Shands for treatment," Cara said.

I turned back to Cyril. "You ever see anyone else hanging out with Timberlane and Gibson?"

"Some of the guys from the community went over when they first showed up, but most of them drifted off eventually. Too much crazy. I saw a couple men that I didn't recognize. I think I saw one guy several different times. A scraggly-looking fellow. He fit in with those two. Looked more like he should be hanging out in the yard at Raiford."

"Hair, height?"

"Dirty red hair, receding in front. Not too tall. Shorter than me. I'm 5'11". I think he was Gibson's friend 'cause I saw them together a couple times without Timberlane. We'd already established the fact that we weren't going to be friends, so they didn't exactly introduce me to him."

"What kind of car?"

"That I remember. Real old little red pickup. Said Datsun on the tailgate. Had some Bondo spots on it like he was fixing it up."

We talked for a little longer before Cara and I left. Walking around the circle, Cara pointed out who lived in each of the houses.

"How old are most of the folks here?"

"The owners are mostly Mom and Dad's age. A few of them are younger. But the folks who are passing through, some of them are old and a lot are young. So you think someone from here killed both of them?"

"I don't know. I think it's safe to say the two killings are related since they were both hung, albeit in different ways. The knots looked similar to me, but I'll have the state guys compare them. I think it's safe to say that a man did it."

"You don't think a woman could have killed them?" Her voice held a bit of a challenge.

"Not that. Both of the victims could have been made to do most of the work themselves if the killer had a weapon to threaten them with. No, I was thinking about the phone calls that your father got."

"Good point. I guess you are a good detective," she said, bumping into me playfully.

"We'll get your dad out."

"I know you will."

When we got back to her parents' house she grabbed a map of the co-op from her father's office and wrote in the names of the residents.

"Which one is Ellie's family?" She pointed to one and put a check by it.

"Okay, go ahead and draw a circle around the names of the folks under the age of sixty. Not that it couldn't be someone older, but we want to narrow the field a little. These guys had a thing for women, so let's put a check mark next to women under the age of forty-five. Again, not that older women don't get raped, but we'll start off playing the odds." Cara marked up the map as I talked.

"Put a mark next to Terri's house. I want to ask her parents if she ever said anything to them about Gibson or Timberlane bothering her." She marked a house and wrote *Terri Andrews* next to it.

"That's the best that I can do from memory. I'll ask Teddy tomorrow. He runs the co-op's board. Dad and he have butted heads a few times," she said, looking at her handiwork.

"Which brings us to another aspect of the crimes. Can you think of anyone who has a grudge against your father?"

"Not really. Dad's as stubborn as a mule, and it's not unusual for him to have contests of will with people. Friends and family mostly, but he never lets it get out of hand. I've seen him come home and rant for an hour and then he calls the person he disagreed with and apologizes. Even when he's right."

"The argument with Timberlane?"

"That's different. If he saw Timberlane hurt someone… Dad wouldn't stand for someone being hurt. The only other time I've seen him in real trouble was about ten years ago.

We were helping someone move out of an apartment complex in town. I was upstairs getting some boxes when I heard a guy screaming. I came running out and found Dad holding a puppy. There was a big guy, bigger than Dad, lying in the parking lot cradling his head and whining. Cops showed up about fifteen minutes later. Dad had seen the guy kick the puppy, so he grabbed the guy by his shirt and threw him down on his back. Cops came and one of them took the puppy to a vet. Turned out he'd broken three of the poor thing's ribs. Cops gave the guy a choice: first-degree felony animal abuse, and my dad gets arrested for assault, or everyone just walks away. Not surprisingly, he chose to walk away."

"So you think your dad could have hurt Timberlane?"

"The day Dad caught him grabbing Ellie, yes. In fact, I'm surprised that Dad *didn't* do more. But I don't see him doing anything in cold blood."

She walked me out to the van and we held hands for a few minutes. Finally we said our goodnights with a small kiss and parted.

The light was on in my motel room as I approached the door. No sound came from inside so I assumed that Mauser had finally gone to sleep. When I opened the door I was surprised to see Mrs. Perkins asleep in a chair next to the bed while Mauser was snoring with his head on a pillow. I closed the door loudly and both of them woke up, looking at me with dopey half-asleep looks on their faces.

"Oh, I must have dozed off reading." Mrs. Perkins raised the book in her lap to show me a Nancy Drew title. Mauser crawled across the bed to the foot and yawned, wide and long.

"I really appreciate you looking after him." I meant every word.

"He's such a sweet boy," she said fondly. Mauser rolled over and stretched out his legs.

I picked up his leash and harness. He jumped off the bed, ready for his late night "walkies." Mrs. Perkins waved as she headed back to her place. There was a small cottage on the other side of the main building that I assumed was her residence.

I called Chavez early the next morning. "I'd like to search the Gibson trailer for anything that might relate to the Tyler murder," I said, trying to sound as business-like as possible. "And interview some of the locals."

"Our crime scene people got what they needed from the trailer. I'll meet you out there and you can take what you need. I'll just make a note of it," Chavez told me. I'd hoped that he'd let me go in on my own, but I could have figured that wasn't going to happen.

The day was going to be cool and cloudy so I packed Mauser a bag for the day and loaded him into the van. He could help me interview people. Actually, I was learning that having Mauser along was a good way to get someone to let down their guard.

I met Chavez at the trailer and pretended that I'd hadn't already been there once. I looked through the place again, finding the duct tape in due course.

"We looked at that, but it wasn't even close to what was used on our victim. Different brand."

"May not match ours either," I said, bagging it up. "Worth checking though."

Locking up the trailer, Chavez asked me who I wanted to interview. I showed him the map that Cara had made up the night before and explained the various marks. "I asked Laursen's daughter to mark this up for me."

He looked at the map. "I had deputies talk to these folks yesterday, right after we identified the body." He pointed to several houses that were closest to Gibson's, including Cyril Riggs's. Which was good because I didn't want to run the risk of Riggs letting on that I'd been there the night before.

We agreed we'd do in-depth interviews with five of the residents today while he had deputies go door to door with the rest, just to make sure that we didn't miss anything. The five we'd picked included Ellie's family; they had to be considered prime suspects. If she told her parents about Tyler grabbing her, then maybe they were angry enough to take out their revenge on him. It seemed a stretch, but it had to be considered. We'd also talk with Terri's folks.

I offered to drive and Chavez accepted before he realized that Mauser would be joining us. He got into the passenger seat and Mauser, wagging his tail excitedly, stuck his face into the front of the van to greet him. I could tell that Chavez was thinking seriously about getting back out when he saw the drool hanging off of Mauser's flews.

I took a few minutes to bring Chavez up to speed on what we had on the Tyler murder. I handed him my iPad to review the crime scene photos. He scanned them, paying particular attention to the rope and knots used.

"Very likely it's the same person, or someone who had a lot of knowledge about the first hanging." He shrugged and handed me back the iPad.

The first house we came to was a log home, rustic but very nicely built. The door was answered by a woman in her late thirties.

"Hello," she said brightly, as though she'd never met a person she didn't like. Kay Landry was tall and blond, her hair pulled back in a ponytail, and wearing a wide smile. She was very attractive in a girl-next-door sort of way. Chavez introduced us. Our profession and purpose for being there got a slight downturn of the lips, but the smile quickly returned.

"I heard about that. The co-op has a very well developed grapevine. It's horrible. I didn't know the man very well, but I'd seen him around. In fact, he'd done some work for my husband."

"Here?" I asked.

"No, John has a small construction company. They build greenhouses and he sometimes needs a few extra hands on a job site."

"Is your husband at home?" Chavez asked.

"No, he pretty much works six days a week unless the weather won't let him." Chavez and I both made a note to talk to the husband first chance we got.

"What interactions did you have with Mr. Gibson?" Chavez was watching her carefully as he asked this question, but there was no noticeable reaction.

"None really. My husband introduced him at one of the co-op's get-togethers. And I saw him around a few times. That was it."

"Did you ever feel like he was being inappropriate?" I asked.

"I don't know what… Oh, I see. No. Nothing like that." She seemed very innocent.

"Did you know a fellow by the name of Doug Timberlane?" I followed up.

Mrs. Landry seemed to think for a moment. "Maybe, there was a guy that did odd jobs for a while. I think that might have been his name. He did some work on the Davis's house. They had some dry rot. They're pretty old and the co-op helps take care of their house. I went over there one day with some figs for them, and he was working on their porch." She said this slowly, as though she was trying to be certain of her memory.

"Anything you can remember about that meeting?"

"Why are you asking about him?" she asked back. It was the first time that she'd seemed reluctant to answer a question.

"He's part of the inquiry into Mr. Gibson's death," I said vaguely, not wanting to color her answer by letting her know that he was dead too.

"Well… It's funny that you should ask about him right after you asked about inappropriate behavior. I don't want to get him into trouble. It was really nothing, but…" She took a deep breath. "It was mostly the way he looked at me. I know how that sounds. But believe me, this was creepy. I've had lots of guys give me the once over. That's one thing, but this was something else. It wasn't that he was looking at something he wanted... More like he was trying to decide whether it was worth taking." She shook herself. "The whole thing weirds me out."

"Did you talk to him at all?" I was hoping for a little more.

"No, I didn't want anything to do with him."

"Did you tell anyone how you felt about him?"

She looked down at the floor. After a long pause, she looked back up at me. "I should have. Usually I'm the one that's pushing people to action. I've worked in women's clinics and told women over and over that you have to speak out when there's a problem. But there wasn't anything I could put my finger on and specifically say he did *this*. It even sounded a bit hysterical in my own head to be worried just by how he looked at me. That's not a fair way to deal with people. But it nagged at me a bit, thinking about him being around other people here at the co-op. But a week later he was gone, so I let it go."

We asked a few more questions which she answered calmly and openly. We asked her to have her husband call us sooner rather than later and left.

Chavez and I discussed the interview as we made our way to the next house on our list. We both felt that she had been honest in her answers and we weren't expecting any great revelations from her husband.

Next up was Ellie's family. They were renting a small cinderblock house. The yard was filled with metal artwork; made from scrap materials, the pieces were clever and interesting. There were several alligators made of metal in different poses with palm trees and palmettos. A small one depicted a gopher tortoise and another was a rattlesnake.

A hissing sound could be heard coming from the side of the house. I followed Chavez, who bypassed the front door and followed the sound around the back of the house to a large pole barn. A short, heavyset man wearing a welding hat and leather apron was using a blowtorch to cut out shapes from an old metal sign. He stopped cutting and stepped back to look at the bear that was forming in the metal, then he noticed us and lifted his visor. He had a dark complexion, with heavy features and black hair.

Chavez spoke Spanish to the man, who answered back. His eyes were dark and serious.

"This is my colleague, Deputy Larry Macklin. He doesn't speak Spanish," Chavez said. The man nodded respectfully at me. "Mr. Zacapa is from Guatemala. His English isn't so good."

They spoke in Spanish for a couple minutes. I recognized Ellie's name, but not much else.

Chavez turned to me. "He's Ellie's father. Henry talked to him about what happened that day. He says he was mad, but he felt that Henry handled it well."

"The man go," Mr. Zacapa said and shrugged.

"Did you tell anyone else in your family about what happened?" I asked and Chavez translated.

Mr. Zacapa thought for a moment. "Madre. Yes. No more."

Chavez asked a question and Mr. Zacapa answered. "He says it's possible that his daughter told someone else, but he doubts it. She was very embarrassed."

When we left, I asked Chavez what he thought about Mr. Zacapa as a suspect. It's hard to judge someone's answers when you don't speak the same language.

"Salt of the earth type. I think he was being honest. If he saw someone hurting a member of his family, he would be capable of hurting or killing them. But in cold blood... No, I don't see it."

CHAPTER FIFTEEN

Our next stop was Terri Andrews's house. Cara had said that her parents might or might not be home, depending on her father's doctor appointments at the hospital. The house was an interestingly formed concrete construction. I'd call it Frank Lloyd Wright meets *Planet of the Apes*. It had an odd appeal to it, seeming to grow up from the ground. We knocked on the hobbit-like wooden door and it was opened by a middle-aged woman with a grim face. But she managed a smile when she saw us.

"Can I help you?" She looked from me to Chavez and back to me.

"We're here about the death of Mr. Gibson," Chavez said.

"Oh, yes, we heard about that. Come in." She stepped back from the door, giving us room to enter. "I don't know how we can help."

She closed the door and led us into the center of the house. The doors to other rooms in the house all opened onto the living area. There were paintings, pictures and wooden carvings everywhere. Only the open nature of the house kept it from feeling too cluttered. It made you think of an art museum where the curator couldn't decide what he liked best.

"Almost all of this is Terri's work," Mrs. Andrews told us.

"Amy, who is it?" came a shout from behind one of the doors.

She headed for the door. "Bill, they're from the sheriff's office. They're here about that man that was killed." She went through the door and in a few moments wheeled her husband out into the living room. Both his legs were missing at the knee and there was a bag hanging beside the chair that suggested urinary issues. He held his left arm at an odd angle to his body.

"I'm Bill and this is my wife, Amy. I don't know what we can tell you. This is our daughter's house. We're just staying here until I get done with the doctors. Or as done as I'm going to get," he said in an attempt at humor.

"I'm sorry. Cara said that you were in an accident?" Too late I realized I'd used Cara's first name too casually and looked over to see if Chavez had noticed. But he was looking sympathetically at Bill.

"Yes. A couple months ago we were on our way here to see Terri. My own stupid fault. Rainy night. I started to fall asleep and jerked the steering wheel, lost control and hit a tree." He reached out and took his wife's hand. "I'm just glad that it was me that got the worst of it." She squeezed his hand, then put her own on the arm of the wheelchair.

"We're talking to a number of the families who live in the co-op."

"Like I said, this is our daughter's house. She's in Italy right now."

"She wanted to stay and help me with Bill, but she'd already been accepted into an art program in Rome. We didn't want her to miss out on that," Amy added.

"Did she mention anything about a man bothering her?"

"What do you mean?" Amy looked at us quizzically.

"A man here at the co-op. Following her? Maybe just making her feel uncomfortable?"

"Noooo, I don't remember her saying anything like that."

"Would she have told you if she was having problems?" Chavez asked.

Bill laughed slightly and took Amy's hand again. "My two girls are as close as a mother and daughter can be. They tell each other everything."

"He's right. She's our only daughter and we've spoiled her. Not that it hurt her. She's a great girl."

"Is there a way that we can contact her?"

Bill and Amy looked at each other. "You can call her cell phone. I'll give you her number," Amy said, going over to the kitchen counter and searching for a piece of paper. "We made sure that she could use her phone overseas." She wrote out the number and offered it to us.

There was an awkward moment when Chavez and I both reached for it. I let him take it. His jurisdiction, after all.

We talked with them for a little while longer, not that we had any good questions to ask, but I think both Chavez and I felt like we needed to stay for a few minutes after disturbing Bill Andrews. He seemed to appreciate visiting with us.

Back in the van, I copied down the number. "What time is it in Rome?" I asked Chavez, who was trying to fend off Mauser.

"Six or seven hours later, maybe."

I dialed the number. After four rings a woman answered. "Hello?"

"Terri Andrews?"

"Yes. Who is this?" She sounded annoyed, or maybe angry.

"I'm Deputy Larry Macklin. I'm calling from Gainesville." I didn't bother explaining that I wasn't an Alachua County deputy.

"Has something happened to my parents?" She sounded very scared.

"No, no, nothing like that. Your parents are fine." I felt stupid for not realizing that might be her first thought after getting a call from a deputy. "In fact, your mother was the one who gave us this number. We're investigating the murders of two men that you might know and we had some questions for you." I put the phone on speaker. "My colleague Lt. Chavez is here with me."

"Murder?"

"Yes, a man named Timberlane and another one named Gibson have been killed."

There was only silence from her end.

"Terri, are you there?"

"Sorry, you said that they had been killed?" She sounded confused. Not surprising if you're running around Rome and suddenly get a call from investigators asking you about two guys you hardly knew back in the States.

"Yes, did you know them?"

"I… don't… Yes, I guess. They lived at the co-op, right?"

"Yes."

"I see. I don't think I can tell you much. I may have met them, but that's all." She sounded sure.

"You don't remember having any trouble with either one of them?"

"Trouble, what kind of trouble?"

"Unwanted attention. Sexual harassment. That type of thing?"

"No, of course not. I have a class in a few minutes. Is that all you needed to know?"

Chavez and I looked at each other. Finally I said, "Yes. But if you remember anything about the men or their interactions with other folks here at the co-op, please call us at this number."

"Okay. I can't imagine what I could know that would help, but I have your number. I need to go now."

"Next," Chavez said.

I pulled into the driveway of a neatly kept doublewide trailer decorated tastefully for the holidays. According to the map it was the home of Karen Gill and her daughter, Andi. Mauser was dancing around in the van so I decided to take him out for a short walk before knocking on the door. Chavez, protests aside, seemed to enjoy Mauser as we walked him around the wooded lot next door.

We heard the door of Karen Gill's house open and close. As we came back to the van, a short, full-bodied woman stood watching us. She smiled at Mauser. "Can I help you all?" she asked in a deep Southern accent.

Chavez went over and explained who we were and why we were there.

"And who's that big boy?" she asked. "Can I pet him?"

I assured her that he'd like nothing better, and then answered all of her questions about him. Finally, having finished the Mauser meet-and-greet, I put him back in the van and gave him a treat.

"It's still pretty cold out here. Let's go inside," Karen offered. We followed her into the house. It was clean, but cluttered with life—coats, books and cat toys. I caught just a glimpse of an orange tabby running toward a back room. I wondered if he'd been watching Mauser through the window.

"I did know both of them. I organize a lot of the community get-togethers. And part of that is making sure that the new people know they're welcome."

"Did you get any unwanted attention from the men?" I asked and thought I saw her tense up.

"What, like flirting?" she asked rather quickly. "Not really. Maybe a suggestive word or two, a look, but I didn't pay much attention. I'm usually running around trying to get everything done. Honestly, I've had relationships where the guys told me that they had wanted to talk to me for months, even years earlier, but they never had the chance. I was either moving too fast or talking too much to give them a chance. Well, I guess you can tell that I'm a bit of a talker. But both of them were nice enough. I wasn't sure if they were going to fit in or not. I've been wrong plenty of times, so I've learned to keep my judgmental side in check."

She stopped talking for a moment and I figured I'd better jump into the gap. I was happy we'd at least found someone else who had talked with Tyler and Gibson. "What can you tell us about your encounters with them?"

"Encounters…" Again I saw a funny look on her face. "That's a fancy word for dropping in and inviting them to a picnic. Let me think. They were pretty friendly at first. The first time I met Mr. Timberlane, he had just moved in a week or so before, and he still had a couple boxes of his stuff sitting in the living room. Gibson was there too. Funny thing was, they seemed like old friends. Not like people who'd just met a week earlier. I even asked if they'd known each other before and they both said no, maybe a little too fast, if you know what I mean. But, like I said, they were real friendly and asked if there would be beer at the picnic. That kind of thing. Now that you mention it, I think Timberlane did wink at me. I didn't think anything of it at the time," she finished, looking away from my eyes.

"You said they were friendly *at first*. Were they not friendly the next time you saw them?" I inquired.

"What…" Karen seemed momentarily confused. "Oh… Oh, no, no, they really weren't, but I thought that was just 'cause I'd interrupted them."

"Interrupted them doing what?" Chavez chimed in. I could tell by the way he was watching her that he'd picked up on the fact she was hiding something.

"They had a friend with them. It was in their front yard. Which is why I was a little surprised they were upset that I stopped to talk to them. If you want privacy, go inside. Right? But they didn't want me there and made it pretty obvious."

"Did you recognize the man that was with them?"

"No. He was short and had receding red hair. Probably in between Timberlane and Gibson in age. Wearing a T-shirt. Wait… The shirt was from a restaurant. I thought at the time that I wouldn't want to eat there if he was the type of employee they hired. Express Burgers, that's it. I got the feeling that he was either going to work or just getting off. The three of them were whispering like girls in the back of class. I told them about a birthday party for one of our older members. They just blew me off."

Chavez and I were both interested in this mysterious third member of the clique. I didn't tell Chavez that Cyril Riggs had described the same man. Secrets. Sooner or later I was going to slip up. I was certainly risking losing Chavez's trust.

"Do you think you could identify this man if you saw him again?" Chavez asked.

"I've got a good memory for faces. I'm sure I could do one of those lineups and pick him out. I would feel bad, but there was so much negative energy coming off those three. I hope I'm not telling tales out of class. But with two of them dead, it sounds like something bad was going on."

"How old is your daughter?"

"Fifteen. Why?"

"Do you think she might have had any run-ins with these men?" Chavez was trying to be delicate, but I saw the look that came over Karen's face. She didn't like the suggestion. The idea seemed to take her by surprise and her face flushed red.

"No. No, she would have said something. We've had that talk several times. Kids, you have to repeat the message at least a dozen times and have them repeat it back to you almost as much before you can believe they've heard and understood what you've told them. I am well aware of what can happen to a woman in this world. My daughter is mature and savvy. If I thought for a minute…"

A look of understanding came over her face. "Oh, I see. Yes, if they had done something to Andi, then I would be your prime suspect. I'd be ashamed if I *didn't* do something." She paused again. "I guess I shouldn't be saying that, but damn it. I… Andi…" Karen's feelings seemed to be muddled up with something besides motherly concern.

"I have children of my own. I think every parent feels the way you do," Chavez said. "It's natural to want to protect them and normal to want to get back at someone who hurts them."

"They were that kind of men?" she asked softly. Again there was something else there. I tried to decipher what it was, but couldn't put my finger on it.

"We think they might have been. Didn't Henry tell you why he'd asked Timberlane to leave?" I asked.

"No. Henry wouldn't. As talkative as I am, Henry isn't. If you want to get gossip out of him, you'd better be prepared to pull it out with a tow truck," she said with half a smile.

"Would you ask your daughter about them and let us know if she has any information?"

We said our goodbyes and Karen walked us out to the van for one more look at Mauser, who managed to haul himself up off his cushy bed and stick his nose out the window.

"I swear that's the biggest dog I've ever seen," she said just before we drove off.

"I want to go check out Express Burgers," I said.

"Yes, me too," Chavez admitted. "Let's finish the last interview." Then he asked, "So what did you think of Ms. Gill?"

"She was hiding something," I stated flatly.

He nodded. "But what? I think we'll have to talk to her again."

After consulting the map, I drove to Reed and Debbie Holly's house. It was a large, rambling wood-framed home with cedar siding tucked back in the woods. Three dogs of various sizes and colors ran out to meet the van. Two of them high-tailed it for the porch when Mauser stood up and gave two thundering barks of greeting out the window. The third dog, a small medium-sized brown and white mix, looked up in adoration at the giant. We got out and were accosted by the dog's nose as she sniffed us up and down, trying to take in as much of Mauser's scent as possible.

A man in a red flannel shirt came out onto the porch and stared at us. "Can I help you?" he yelled.

Chavez pulled out his badge and held it up. "Alachua County Sheriff's Office," he yelled back.

"Oh," was all the man said. We took that for what it was worth and walked up to the house. The other dogs insisted on smelling us when we reached the porch.

"Jesus, what is that thing?" the man, Reed Holly I assumed, asked as he stared at the van. Mauser still had his head sticking out, watching the dogs on the porch. I gave a quick explanation and Reed shook his head. "Are our taxes paying to feed that monster?"

"No, he's not on the payroll. I'm with the Adams County Sheriff's Office, down here investigating a homicide."

We made our introductions and Mr. Holly invited us into the living room where a wood stove was sending out waves of heat. Debbie Holly stood up when we came in. She was a good-looking woman in her forties who must have been stunning in her twenties. I looked back at Reed Holly, who was 5'10" with brown hair going grey around the edges and a rough-hewn face with a nose that was a little small for the rest of his features. He wasn't ugly, but he seemed to be punching above his weight class with Debbie. Uncharitably, I wondered how much money he had.

The Hollys invited us to sit down. As soon as we were all situated, Chavez explained why we were there. When he said Timberlane's name, Reed Holly's face turned beet red. By the time Chavez finished, Reed looked like he wanted to punch something. Debbie noticed and placed her hand on his thigh.

"Mr. Holly, you seem upset. Did you have a run-in with Timberlane?" I asked.

He looked at me for a moment as though he thought he could deny it. "Yes, two actually." He hesitated.

"Want to tell us about them?" Chavez asked.

Reed Holly sighed heavily. "I wish I could say they were

123

nothing, but I was pretty sure they were at the time. I told you we should have reported it to the board, or at least to Henry." This last was directed at his wife. He turned back to us. "Timberlane was here doing some work on the side of the house. I should have done the work myself, but I was busy and didn't want to let the dry rot go. Anyway, he was working and I had to go out to mail some packages. Long and short of it, I found him inside the house in my office. He made some stupid excuse about needing to use the bathroom and getting lost. I told him to leave and that I'd finish the work myself."

"What did he do then?" Chavez asked.

"He was mad. He got right in my face and stared into my eyes. But what could he do? Finally he left, but not without slamming the door and giving it an extra kick. I thought that was the end of it until… Debbie, you tell this part of it since it happened to you."

"Okay." She sounded very uncomfortable. "I was jogging through the neighborhood. I usually try to get in a couple miles every other day or so. Anyway, this was a few months ago, and I was on my second loop. I went by the rental trailers. Timberlane was doing something with his car. When I ran by he looked up and stared. It was odd… Lust mixed with disgust, if that makes any sense. It creeped me out so much that I decided to head straight back to the house. I was almost done anyway. I made it home okay and got cleaned up, but when I came downstairs I heard the dogs barking. When I looked out, I saw someone pass by one of the windows. I was already spooked and this freaked me out."

"What happened next?"

"I got the gun we keep in the nightstand and then I called Reed," she said flatly.

"Unfortunately I was out of town. I told her to call 911."

"But while I was still on the phone with Reed, I looked out the window and saw Timberlane walking around the house."

"And I told her to fire a round out the window at the

bastard." Reed was visibly reliving his anger and anxiety.

"I didn't think I should shoot at him. But I thought about that look he'd given me and I opened the window and told him to get the hell away from our house. I shot the gun at the ground."

"Did he leave?"

"He looked up at me like he was trying to decide how serious I was. I just held the gun and stared back at him. Finally, I swear it felt like an hour but was probably only a couple of minutes, he left."

"Did you call 911?" Chavez asked.

"I was getting ready to when one of the neighbors called. I told him a little bit about what had gone on and he said he'd be right over. He's older, but was in the Marines. Ten minutes later he knocked on the door, said he'd checked around the house and Timberlane was gone. He called his wife up and the three of us wound up having a movie night here. They even slept over in the guest room."

"I was home by noon the next day. We talked about it. I called Teddy, who's on the board, and asked him what was going on with Timberlane. He said that a couple people had made complaints and that they were deciding what to do. I told him I'd vote to kick him off the island. Teddy didn't ask for details, and I didn't offer them. I wish I had now." Again Debbie patted his leg.

We went over some more of the details with them and then headed for the door. One of the difficulties with interviewing people is knowing whether their emotions are caused by the questions you're asking or by events that happened before the interview began. Reed was on edge. Why? Was it just our questions?

I left feeling like we failed to find something that they were hiding. But one of the first lessons you learn is that a hunch can be wrong. *A feeling can be deceiving* was what my field training officer used to say. I talked it out with Chavez and he agreed we'd revisit them if nothing else panned out.

CHAPTER SIXTEEN

It was past noon when we drove into the parking lot of the nearest Express Burgers. I took Mauser for a walk in the grass alongside the restaurant, gave him water and fed him his lunch. With the air full of the smell of grilled burgers, he was less than impressed with his dry food.

"My children are not as much work as that dog," Chavez said with a chuckle.

In the restaurant we asked for the manager, who turned out to be a young man with a sour demeanor. The permanent sneer on his face perfectly accented his small hooded eyes. My first thought was that he was the last person on God's green earth I'd want to work for.

"Yeah, what can I do for you?" he asked after we'd shown him our badges. "I hope this is about the vandalism a couple of weeks ago. I didn't think that the officer who took the report seemed like he was taking it very seriously."

"I'm afraid this isn't about the vandalism. We're looking for a man that might work for you. We need to question him about an incident. Right now we are not considering him a suspect," Chavez said, which was kind of true and kind of a lie.

"Yeah, okay. Who are you looking for? We get a lot of

turnover here." The manager, Donnie according to his name tag, was clearly not interested in our investigation. *Jerk*, I thought.

"We don't have a name. He's got red hair with a receding hair line, he's under 5'9", he's in his early thirties. Drives a Datsun pickup truck." Chavez rattled off the list.

"What kind of truck?"

"A Datsun. They changed their name to Nissan about twenty years ago. So we're talking about an old, small pickup truck. Has a lot of Bondo on it."

"Has what?" This guy was clearly not a gearhead.

"Places on the truck where the body was repaired. It'd look like big white spots," I explained.

"Oh." That was it. Just "oh" as if he'd forgotten we'd asked a question.

"Do you know who we're talking about? Did he ever work for you?" Chavez said it slowly and calmly.

"Maybe."

"You don't know?"

"There was a guy kinda like that, but he didn't work here long. Maybe a month." He took out his phone and idly played with it—sending a text, checking his email, updating his Facebook status. Who knew?

Disgusted, I reached out and took the phone from him. He seemed surprised, but didn't put up any resistance.

"What we're asking is very important. You need to concentrate and answer our questions fully and accurately. Now could you please check your records, ask some of the other employees or do whatever else you need to do to give us a name and contact information for this guy?"

"Can I have my phone back?" he asked with a petulant expression.

"After you get the information we need," I said. He stared at me like he didn't know how to handle someone telling him what to do.

"Do it now," Chavez and I said in unison.

Donnie turned around to the employees who were

actually working their asses off serving customers and shouted, "Hey, what was the name of the guy who drove that old shitty truck? He had nasty red hair. Guy was like thirty. Old."

"Billy something… Oh, yeah, Billy Good. Which was funny because there wasn't anything good about him," answered a girl at the counter without looking up from her cash register. *And she has to work for this idiot,* I thought.

"Billy Good," the manager parroted.

I held up his phone. "Could you check your employment records and give us his contact information?"

"Hey, don't you need a warrant or something?" Of course he didn't care about any legalities, he just wanted his phone back and didn't want to be bothered.

"No," Chavez and I said again. Remarkably, we were well within bounds to lie. If a suspect or witness believes you, that's on them. I try not to make it a rule, but it can be damn handy sometimes.

He turned around and we followed him into the cramped cubbyhole that served as an office. He dropped into a chair and started fiddling with the keyboard, eyes glued to the computer screen.

"Yeah, William Good. Here it is."

I reached out and shifted the monitor, taking several pictures of the screen with my phone. We thanked him and left as fast as we could.

"I was hungry before we went in there," Chavez said.

I apologized to Mauser for not bringing him a burger. Chavez and I overcame our post-Express Burgers queasiness and stopped at a sandwich shop to grab a quick bite before heading to the address listed on Good's application.

"That address probably won't be any good. I'll run his name, see what we get," Chavez offered. He was able to access the system through his phone.

"Surprise, surprise, that's his real name. He's got mostly minor stuff. Spent six months here and a year there in county lock-ups for drug- and alcohol-related offenses.

There was an assault charge for a family fight, apparently, and a couple of small-time burglaries. Nothing with a gun. That's good news for us. Unfortunately, he's not on parole so the only 'current' address we have is his driver's license, which matches the employment application."

The address was in an older neighborhood built up in the post-World War II housing boom. The houses were starter homes, three-bedroom, two-bath models on quarter-acre lots. Some were now rented out to students, others were serving as starter homes for the current generation, and a few housed retirees.

Good's house didn't look like a rental. The yard was neat and there were only two vehicles in the driveway. The garage had been bricked up and converted into an addition years ago.

"We just won the missing witness lottery," Chavez said when we saw that Good's old pickup was the second car in the driveway. We parked behind it and went up to the door, which had a large faded Christmas wreath in the middle of it. A fairly well dressed woman in her sixties answered the doorbell.

"Cops," she stated without surprise. "He's in his room. Come in." She turned and we followed her into the living room. The house was bright and well kept.

"Billy! Get out here!" she yelled. After a couple moments, we heard a noise from the side of the house. She turned to us. "He's going out the window. He'll come around the front of the house if you want to catch him. He's not as fast as he used to be." Before she finished, Chavez and I were heading back out the front door.

We got outside in time to see Good, wearing an open flannel shirt, jeans and no shoes, pass us on his way across the lawn. He must have hoped he'd be able to escape in his truck. When he saw that we had him blocked in, he turned left and started past my van. Mauser must have been watching the excitement because he chose just the right moment to jump at his open window, giving out one of his seismically measured barks. Billy Good screamed, lost his footing and tumbled to the ground. I caught up with him and placed my knee on his back, pinning him to the ground. I looked back for Chavez and saw him down on his knees, laughing hysterically.

"Oh, my, that was the best ever! Dear God, if we had gotten that on video we would own the Internet for a week." He collapsed into another fit of laughter.

I turned back to Good, who was squirming under me, trying to get a look at the monster in the van who was looking happily down at us.

"Why'd you run?"

"What the hell is that thing? That's the biggest damn dog I've ever seen. Jesus!"

"Are you done running? If so, I'll let you up. Try to run again and we'll haul you in." We didn't have any reason to haul him in, and running from law enforcement officers who haven't even told you to stop or identified themselves isn't a crime anywhere in this country, but again, that lying thing can come in handy.

"I won't run. What the hell are you all harassing me for? I haven't done nothing."

I let him up.

"Then why were you running? You forget that you're innocent?" Chavez asked. He'd finally stopped laughing and caught up with us.

"Man, you all are always busting my ass."

"We just want to ask you a few questions."

"Damn, it's cold out here."

I stepped between him and the street. "Maybe your mother will let us sit inside and talk."

"That old battle-ax. Maybe." He started shuffling barefoot to the front door, with Chavez flanking him and me behind him so he couldn't make another run for the street.

His mother opened the door. After we were all inside, she closed the door and muttered, "Dumbass. Make yourselves at home. I'm going in the back. I don't need to hear any more of his crap." She disappeared down the hall.

We all sat and looked at each other for a minute before Chavez started us off. "Your name is Billy Good. You're friends with Thomas Gibson and Doug Timberlane. What can you tell us about your relationship with them?"

"Oh, shit. Someone killed Tommy. I heard about that. Damn, man. I've known Tommy since high school." He shook his head and looked down at the floor. "It sucks," he added, in case we didn't realize that being dead was a bad thing.

"You know Doug Timberlane too." Chavez was posing the questions as statements to push Good to tell us the truth. Or at least to skip the early lies that he was going to tell us and allow us to get straight to the rest of the lies.

"I don't know," he said very tentatively, trying to see if there was any wiggle room.

"You, Gibson and Timberlane were all seen together at the co-op north of town."

"Oh, yeah, he was a friend of Tommy's. We just hung out a couple of times."

"What did you all do when you 'hung out'?" Chavez asked.

Good shrugged.

"That's not good enough. We need to know what you all were doing. You should realize that your ass is on the line here."

"We watched football, worked on my truck, smoked a little weed. That's all." He looked sad, as if the world was picking on him.

"Where were you yesterday morning?" Chavez delivered the question with force.

Billy Good looked up with a surprised expression on his face. "You don't think I had anything to do with Tommy's murder?" His voice was high and incredulous. He was really shocked that we had gone there.

"Just answer my question." Chavez's voice was low and menacing.

"I was here. Ask my mom. I don't get up until noon, usually. Really. I scored... I got some stuff and was pretty gone by, like, one o'clock. I got high, played *Armored War* and fell asleep. End of story, man."

As stupid as his alibi was, I believed it and I could tell that Chavez did too. This idiot didn't have the smarts to pull off that type of murder and frame Henry.

"You say that Doug Timberlane was Tommy's friend," I said, imitating Chavez's interview technique.

"Yeah, but there's something funny about that. Tommy didn't call him Doug. He called him something else. Dave, that's right, he called him Dave when no one else was around. Dave, Doug, whatever his name was, bragged he was wanted and had to use a fake ID. He's a creepy guy. You know, *he* might have killed Tommy." He seemed excited by his theory. "Yeah, he could have done it. Dave had some killer eyes."

"Did you ever see him hurt anyone?" I asked.

"No," Billy said, way too fast. This was the first deliberate lie he'd told us. I'd come back to it.

"Do you know how Tommy and Dave met?"

"I think in prison, or just after one or both of them got out of prison." He was glad to get away from the question of Dave's violent acts.

"Do you know why someone would murder Tommy?"

"Drugs. Probably drugs."

"Tommy dealt drugs?" Chavez stepped in.

"He grew a little weed. Sold some. But there are guys around here that don't want no one growing their own, if you know what I mean. Could have been something like that."

"You said that you thought Dave could have killed Tommy. Why would he want to do that?" I asked.

"I don't know. He had this temper. Got real mad at people, quick. But it might have been the drug thing."

"What, Dave might have killed him for drugs?"

"No, no, some other guys might have killed Tommy

because of drugs, that's what I mean." Billy really wanted us to get away from questions about Dave.

"Let's stick to Dave. Who did he get mad at?" I asked.

"Oh, I don't know…" His voice trailed off.

"I think you do. Come on, we're talking about Tommy's murder. You want to help us, don't you?"

"Well, yeah, I've known Tommy forever."

"So who did Dave get mad at?"

"Some guy."

"What guy? Come on, you're pissing me off," Chavez said. We were doing a great job going back and forth with our questions and it was beginning to rattle Billy.

"Some guy! I don't know. Dave did some work for the guy. Said the guy was an asshole and kicked him out of his house. Later, he laughed about the guy's wife shooting at him. Why don't you ask him?" Watching and listening to him, I was pretty sure that he didn't know that Tyler was dead.

"It would be easier to talk to him if he wasn't dead," Chavez said with a heavy dose of snark.

Billy looked stunned. You could almost see the gears in his head working this one over.

"So you see our problem. Your little threesome is now a onesome." Chavez leaned forward and captured Billy's eyes with his. "I think this will play out in one of two ways. One, you're a murderer or had something to do with their deaths or, two, you're going to be the next victim. Either case, for your own good, I'd suggest you tell us everything you know about the three of you." Chavez finished and leaned back.

"Why would anyone kill me?" Billy asked in a small voice.

"I don't know, Billy. Why would someone kill your pal Gibson? Why would they kill Timberlane?" I asked him.

"Maybe the same person didn't kill both," Billy squeaked.

"It's possible, but unlikely. I think it's safe to say they're related. And besides the way in which they were killed, there is one other common link between Timberlane and Gibson. You."

"I don't know anything!" Again too fast, an obvious lie.

"I don't believe you," I said.

"They did stuff. I wasn't a part of it. I was just... there," he said lamely.

"Tell us about this stuff they did," Chavez shot back.

"No." Billy stood up. "I don't know anything about their murders."

Chavez stood up too. "Listen to me carefully. What you do now is important. Talk to us. Tell us what we need to know and you can save yourself a lot of grief. If you don't cooperate, then we can't help you."

"I got to think. I don't want to talk anymore."

"I don't think you have a lot of time, Billy. One way or another we're going to figure things out on our own, in which case we aren't going to feel very generous toward you. Any crimes that you might have committed, we'll prosecute to the full extent of the law. *Or* whoever is going around killing your friends is going to realize you're next on his list."

"You could be lying about everything. Just trying to trap me." He was scared and becoming petulant.

"True. Or we're telling you the truth and your window of opportunity is closing." Chavez took out his card. "Call me if you want to talk and aren't dead."

"You need to tell us everything you know, the sooner the better," I said, also handing him one of my cards.

He looked back and forth at us.

"Last chance," Chavez said.

"I'm not talking. Not now," Billy said. He was twitching anxiously. I was pretty sure that the first thing he was going to do when we left was score some drugs.

CHAPTER SEVENTEEN

Back in the van, Chavez and I compared notes.

"We're on to something with this one," Chavez said. "I'll get one of my guys to sit on him. Won't be 24/7, but enough to put some pressure on him. Hopefully our killer won't hit him before he talks to us."

"He was pretty scared."

"They did something that he's afraid to admit. Unfortunately, he's been around the block enough times that he knows how to clam up. The problem is we don't have anything on him right now. I'll tell my guy to keep an eye out and try to get him carrying enough drugs to threaten him with some serious jail time. That might loosen his tongue."

"You rethinking Henry Laursen as the murderer?" I asked nonchalantly.

He looked over at me. "Maybe. But all the evidence is still pointed directly at Laursen. It makes it hard for me to make a case for someone else to be the murderer. Don't you agree?"

"Yes," I said reluctantly. "But I find it hard to believe that Henry did it. The motive is too thin. For killing Tyler... maybe. Thinks he's a scumbag and has to give him money he doesn't think he should have, gets in a fight with him and is mad enough to kill him. Maybe. But Gibson? He didn't see Gibson do anything. In Henry's eyes, Gibson's guilt was based on association with Tyler."

"I agree. But he had the means and opportunity for both and a motive, however thin, for committing both murders. Maybe when he was torturing Tyler he learned something that put Gibson in his crosshairs," Chavez said.

I'd thought about that too. It was a possibility, and all I had to fall back on was that he was Cara's father and therefore he couldn't have done it. That logic wasn't going to get me very far with Chavez.

"Have you checked in with your girlfriend, Cara, today?" Chavez quietly dropped this little bomb. I didn't know what to say.

"Secrets seldom stay secret. I had one of my guys keeping an eye on the co-op last night. He saw the two of you walking hand in hand. Very romantic."

"I'd say it's not what you think, but it probably is," I said lamely.

"You insulted my intelligence. And showed you weren't very clever," he said in a calm, disappointed voice.

"I wasn't trying to be deceptive. I—"

He held up a hand to stop me.

"Of course you were trying to deceive me. But you thought it was for a good cause. I'm not sure that I disagree with you. I don't want to clear cases by putting the wrong person in jail. I want to solve murders by putting guilty people in jail. Henry?" He shrugged his shoulders. "Evidence says yes. Instinct says no. So I want to keep my mind open and keep digging. Hopefully, you'll prove useful." He said this in an easygoing manner. I began to relax.

"What you're doing is very foolish. You're walking a very thin line between helping someone you care about and obstructing justice," he said, not telling me anything I didn't already know. "And the temptations for you in a situation like this could be very great."

I felt like a kid being shamed by his parents. "I

understand."

"Let me ask you a question. Could you be convinced of Henry's guilt?"

"If I saw clear proof, yes."

"What would you consider 'clear proof'?"

"I don't know," I answered honestly.

"Fair enough. And let me be honest with you. If I suspect for even one minute that you are interfering in any way with this investigation, I will have you barred from having anything to do with it. And if I find out you tampered with evidence or did anything else illegal, I'll have you arrested and charged. Are we clear?"

"Yes."

"Good. Take me back to my car. I'll check over the reports and let you know if there is anything interesting in them. I should have a preliminary autopsy report by now and copies of witness interviews. You can come down to the office later and help me look through CCTV footage."

I dropped him off and went to see Cara. At least I didn't have to sneak around anymore. Apparently I wasn't very good at sneaking around anyway.

She answered the door looking tired, but she seemed cheered up at the sight of Mauser.

"You're a tonic for everything that ails me," she said, ruffling his ears and encouraging him to lean into her. She scratched him for a few minutes. I tried not to be jealous of the big goof. He *did* have a way of making you smile whether you wanted to or not.

"Mom's not dealing with this. We *did* find a lawyer that both Mom and Dad could agree on. Hopefully he's meeting with Dad now." All of this poured out of her as we sat down in the living room. "I need to go back to work on Monday. What am I going to do?"

I could see her mother in the backyard, puttering around with some wood project. Cara followed my gaze.

"Exactly. She's told me half a dozen times that we don't have to worry because everything will work itself out. When I asked her why she thought that, she said that Dad had built up enough good Karma for a dozen people. She's taking denial to a new level. The only saving grace is that no one else in the co-op believes Dad did it either. We had a dozen people come by with food for us. Do you want some gluten-free lemon cake?" She smiled a little. "Oh, and Karen Gill came by to tell us about the detectives that had been at her house asking questions. She thought you were very nice. I didn't tell her that I knew you."

"Did she say anything else?" I thought it curious that she came by.

"Actually, she asked *me* questions more than anything," Cara said.

"Questions about what?"

"Why the police suspected Dad. If it was true that Timberlane and Gibson had been harassing women." Cara looked at me oddly. "Why are you interested in Karen?"

"It's probably nothing. Do you know her very well?"

"A little. She's been active in the co-op since she came here about six years ago. More of a guy's girl than a girl's girl, if you get my drift."

"How's that?"

"You know, a bit catty where other women are concerned and maybe a little too flirtatious with men."

"Chavez found out that we're friends," I said, changing the subject.

"How'd that go?"

"Better than I had any right to expect."

"I'm sorry I got you into all of this."

"The sad thing is that I'm grateful it brought us back together." I reached out and took her hand.

She looked down at the floor. "I was a little unfair before. Not being a cop wouldn't guarantee that you wouldn't have to deal with crap."

"I told you then that I understood. There's a lot of

baggage that goes along with dating a deputy. And I appreciate the fact that you thought enough of me that you wanted to make sure it was something you were comfortable with before we got too involved."

"I think you're giving me more credit than I deserve. I can be a little selfish. I'm afraid of sharing my guy with his job, or worse, to take a chance of losing him. But now I'm watching my mother and father and I'm seeing what I should have seen before. Life is dangerous. And you can't be like my mom. You can't pretend it's not, or think that because you do everything right that you don't have to fight for the good things in life when the bad times come knocking on the door."

She had moved over next to me and now she leaned against my shoulder. "I'm willing to give us a shot if you are. This is quite a test for you since my family is in the middle of such a mess right now."

"I'm not worried. I'm glad that I have the chance to help you all through this." I leaned into her and we sat there supporting each other until Mauser came over and tried to sit on my lap. You can't ignore him. I pushed him off and got up.

"I need to go meet Chavez and look through a million hours of video footage from banks, minute markets and traffic cameras. As much footage as we can find from the couple of miles around the park." She nodded and walked Mauser and me out to the van.

The shadows were getting long and the temperature dropping as I drove back to our motel. I fed Mauser his dinner and took him for a long walk. Walking a normal dog is relaxing and gives you a chance to think; walking Mauser gives you an opportunity to have your arms pulled out of their sockets. Every smell is the best smell he's ever gotten a whiff of and you only have two options—follow him and the scent or get pulled to your knees. I made up my mind right then that I was going to set aside some time to work with him. It was only fair to the dog that *someone* take the time.

I called Dad when we got back to the room.

"Larry, hey!" he answered, sounding weirdly upbeat. "How's it going in Gainesville? Chavez should be a good guy to work with."

"He is, actually."

"And how are things going with your girlfriend?" He couldn't resist ribbing me.

"Except for the part where her father is still at the top of everyone's murder suspect list, Cara and I are getting along fine," I answered, irrationally irritated that he seemed so… happy. I was much more used to hearing him when he was in a foul mood, about to be in a foul mood, or just getting over being in a foul mood. I wasn't sure how to take him sounding like Florida's version of Andy Griffith.

He didn't answer and for a minute I thought the call had been dropped. "Dad?"

"Do you know the real reason I asked you to become a deputy when I ran for sheriff?" he finally asked.

Because you wanted to control me, I almost said, but I bit my tongue. More diplomatically, "I figured you just wanted me to follow in your footsteps."

"No, I asked you to join the department because I knew you were smart and clever and would be a damn good deputy."

"Have you been drinking?" It wasn't a very nice thing to say, but it came out before I could stop myself.

"No… Well, a little… Not that much. Forget it. Put Mauser on."

The next few minutes consisted of me holding the phone next to Mauser's head while trying not to hear the ridiculous baby talk coming from the other end. Finally Mauser raised his head and gave Dad a short gruff bark. Figuring it was time to end the conversation, I said, "I need to get some sleep."

"I might go talk to this attractive major from Broward

County. She smiled at me a couple times during a seminar and made a point of telling me she was going to check out the specialty drinks at the bar tonight."

"Now you're just grossing me out."

"Ha! Stay safe," he said and disconnected.

I wondered if I should have told him about Matt. It wouldn't be fair to tell him when both of us were out of the county and couldn't do anything to follow up. On the other hand, was it fair *not* to tell him? I was coming to the conclusion that secrets aren't all the fun they're cracked up to be.

I stopped by the front office and asked Mrs. Perkins if she'd mind looking in on Mauser. You'd have thought I'd given her a winning lotto ticket. Then I grabbed a bite to eat and headed over to the sheriff's office where Chavez and I tried to destroy our eyesight by looking at hours upon hours of oddly lit, grainy CCTV footage.

We were looking for anything that was familiar—a car, a person or someone carrying a sign that read *I'm on my way to kill someone*, or alternatively *I'm going home after killing someone*. But we found nothing. I made a dozen notes of odd cars or people doing something out of the ordinary, like running past or turning away from a camera. When we had a clear suspect we could come back and recheck the footage.

At three o'clock I headed back to the motel. Mauser was sleeping soundly and Mrs. Perkins was nowhere to be found. I got a hot shower and went straight to bed.

Chavez, who apparently never slept or took a day off, called me at eight o'clock the next morning to let me know that he had some of the preliminary crime scene reports, if I wanted to take a look. I stumbled out of bed, dressed, took care of Mauser, then left him in Mrs. Perkins's capable hands for the day.

Chavez let me use a desk in a conference room to go over the reports. Or at least the reports that he didn't mind me looking through. I was confident that he was keeping some evidence back. Any lead investigator on a homicide would. He didn't know how much he could trust me and, honestly, I hadn't proven very trustworthy so far.

After I'd had a chance to go through everything he'd given me, he came in and sat down.

"So?" he asked.

I sighed. "Nothing rules Henry out."

"Exactly. No extra fingerprints on the knife. The knife can't be ruled out as the one used to cut the rope. The rope found in his truck superficially matches the rope around my victim's neck. Without blood evidence, and there were no cuts on the victim or Henry, there is no chance of matching blood. DNA is going to take weeks, maybe months. That leaves us with a big question mark where Henry is concerned." He tapped a large pile of interviews. "And none of the potential witnesses gave us anything beyond the facts we already had." He turned his hands palms up. "What do I do?"

"Honestly, I would let the suspect go. Work on other suspects while I wait for the DNA tests to come back. He's unlikely to flee. You might find a new suspect or the DNA might confirm contact between the original suspect and the victim. Also, you give Henry, your prime suspect, time to do something stupid like get drunk at a bar and run his mouth, go after someone else or try to get rid of evidence you didn't even know about."

"Exactly what I was thinking. He remains a person of interest. I will tell him not to leave the county without notifying me and you can rest assured that I will be watching him."

"I want you to be watching him. The killer was targeting him too," I said with all sincerity. Chavez nodded his head.

It was one o'clock before I left the station and called Cara with the good news. After checking on Mauser and feeding him lunch, I picked up Cara and her mom and drove to the county jail. By four o'clock, Henry was home.

"Thank you," Cara said, hugging me.

"He's not out of the woods yet. Until we know who the killer is, your father is going to be the prime suspect. Plus, the killer is obviously focused on your father. I'm convinced that the murderer is someone from the co-op, or someone with intimate knowledge of it."

My phone rang with a number I didn't recognize. Standing there with Cara, I was tempted not to answer. But I'm not really good at ignoring a ringing phone. She told me to take it the second time I looked at the screen.

The voice on the other end of the line was hushed and breathless.

"What?"

"I need help. Like now."

"Who is this?" Something told me this wasn't a sales call.

"Billy!" he said in a shouted whisper. "You gave me your card. You're a cop, right? But not from around here?"

"What's the trouble? Where are you?"

"I'm out in the woods. Someone's stalking me." His voice was sizzling with paranoia.

"Call 911."

"No, I can't." Near hysterics.

"Why not?"

"I'm in the woods. I'm… Look, I need help… I'm at Tommy's pot spot. Where he grew his weed."

"Why can't you call the cops?" I still didn't quite see the problem.

"Because… He's not the only one growing stuff out here. I get the cops in this and I'll have a hundred people trying to kill me. But you aren't from here. You don't have juris…something."

"Jurisdiction." The logic of a drug addict. "Yeah, sure, that's right. I don't care about the pot." This was probably nothing more than a paranoia-fueled anxiety attack, in which case it might be the perfect opportunity to befriend the idiot and get some information out of him. "I'm on my way. Stay on the line. I need you to tell me how to get there."

I looked at Cara and mouthed, *I have to go. It's Billy Good.*

143

She nodded and I headed out the door.

CHAPTER EIGHTEEN

Billy directed me northwest of town into a rural area of rolling farmland and dense oak woods. Ten miles outside of Gainesville he had me turning onto a series of dirt roads. I crossed a set of railroad tracks and a couple creeks. The only houses now were old trailers that had seen much better days.

Suddenly Billy's voice was gone. I couldn't be sure if my phone or his had dropped the call. I tried calling him back, but he didn't pick up. Luckily he'd given me pretty good directions for the last few miles.

At last I saw his truck. There were no other cars, but there were half a dozen side roads and paths that you could go down and be out of sight after a hundred feet. I understood why growers would choose to plant out here. It was a maze where you could hide or ambush someone easily.

Billy had said he was near a railroad bridge. I had less than an hour before it would be dark and I couldn't get Billy back on the phone. Not having much of a choice, I called Chavez.

"What?" he said after I'd given him the basics. "How the hell? Figures it would be the one time our car had to answer another call. Damn it!"

I used the map on my phone and told him where I was.

"Got it. I'll be there shortly."

As I made my way down the path in the direction Billy had indicated, I had to watch where I was putting my feet as I looked for signs of Billy or his stalker. I knew from some of the drug interdiction work I'd done in the panhandle that growers often put out booby traps to keep weed poachers away from their patch.

I came to the steep sandy bank of a creek. The trail turned and followed the creek north. Up ahead I could make out a bridge. It appeared and disappeared as the trail wound its way along the bank. As I jogged closer I realized that it was an old fashioned, truss-style railroad bridge with four-foot steel sides, rising thirty feet over the shallow creek.

When I was two hundred feet away my heart began to beat faster; there was someone standing in the middle of the bridge. Something was around his neck and the person had red hair. I was running now. Fifty feet from the bridge I heard the sound of a train whistle.

Billy was trying to talk, but there was duct tape over his mouth. I was on the tracks now. The bridge was only a hundred feet across, but I couldn't run on the damn ties. Moving as fast as I could was not fast enough. I heard the train whistle again and this time I could feel the train coming.

Billy's hands and arms were duct-taped to his sides. A thick rope around his neck was tied to a bridge truss. His eyes were pleading with me to hurry. The tracks were beginning to vibrate from the approaching train.

Moving forward, I tried to formulate a plan of escape once I cut Billy free, forcing my mind to stay calm and focused. The bridge was too narrow to stand on and let the train pass. We would have to jump. I didn't need to look to know that the train was already too close to allow us to get across the bridge.

As I reached Billy, I pulled out my pocket knife. It wasn't a big knife. Not nearly big enough. And there wasn't enough time. The train was in sight. I knew that not because I took the time to look, but because I could see Billy's eyes grow huge as he saw it approaching over my shoulder. Apparently the conductor saw us too, as the sound of the whistle screaming took my breath away. A split second later the sound of the locomotive's brakes competed with the deafening horn.

I cut one of Billy's hands free and started sawing at the noose. He ripped the tape off his mouth as I turned my head to see the train too close, sparks flying, barely slowing down. It was jump or die. Rope still around his neck, Billy started to climb over the steel wall. I clambered up beside him, trying to help him balance on the narrow rail. The vibrating bridge doomed Billy. He over-balanced, grabbing onto me as he went and taking both of us over and down.

I reached out, clutching onto him for a second before I realized what that would mean. Yes, he would die anyway from the rope, but I couldn't allow myself to hang onto his dying body to slow my fall. I spread my arms and tried to gauge my fall. All too late. I hit the creek bed hard. Pain shot up my left leg as I rolled onto my side. I splashed and dragged myself to the bank. Looking up, I saw Billy hanging from the bridge, no longer struggling.

After taking a minute to catch my breath, I pulled out my phone, dried it as best I could and called Chavez. Miracle of technology, it worked. I told him briefly what had happened and where I was.

"I'm ten minutes away. I'm calling for backup." I could hear him calling dispatch and telling them there was an officer down.

I lay back in the sand and closed my eyes, feeling my left foot swell. That lasted all of one minute until I remembered that there was a killer on the loose. Someone had duct-taped Billy and put that noose around his neck. They might still be around. I felt for my gun and pulled it out of the holster. The sun was going down and the shadows under the trees were deepening. I listened and didn't hear anything. Finally I crawled up the sandy embankment and back onto the trail.

How long had it been since I had talked to Chavez? Time was moving at an odd pace. Adrenaline can do that to you. Five minutes maybe? I had another five before backup would arrive. I limped back toward the van. I had no idea how the killer had gotten out there, but it was possible they also had a vehicle hidden away somewhere.

By the time I reached the van I could hear sirens approaching. I hadn't seen or heard anyone else nearby. I re-holstered my gun so the deputies arriving on the scene of an "officer down" call didn't find a wet ragged man carrying a gun. I wasn't in my own county where the arriving officers would recognize me.

I was beginning to feel the cold. I'd gotten drenched in the creek and now, with the temperature falling into the forties and the adrenaline wearing off, I was starting to shake. I took out my badge and held it up as the first cars slid to a stop behind my van. Chavez was the first officer out of his car.

"Are you all right?"

"Yeah, basically. The body is that way, on the bridge." He nodded and started issuing instructions to his men while I hobbled over to the van.

"An ambulance is on the way," Chavez told me. He took my wet coat from me and gave me a dry one from his car. Then he knelt down beside me and pulled off my hiking boot, flexing my foot carefully with a professional's touch. Pain surged up my leg.

"Shit, that hurts," I said. "We can just wait for the ambulance."

"I was an EMT for a year before I decided that I wanted to solve crimes and not just cart off the bodies. I don't think there's any major damage," he said.

The ambulance arrived as I called Mrs. Perkins.

"I've had something come up and won't be back to the motel for a few hours. Would you mind feeding Mauser for me?" I hesitated asking her to walk him, but she offered. "That would be great, if you think you can handle him."

"I love big dogs. He and I get along great. What do you want me to tell him about you being late?" I thought she was kidding at first, but as the silence drew out I realized she was serious.

"Um, just tell him I'll be back as soon as I can. Thanks." I hung up, shaking my head.

The EMT confirmed Chavez's initial assessment of my injuries. "Pretty sure it's just a bad sprain, but you really ought to come to the hospital for an X-ray, just to be sure."

That was the last thing I wanted to do. "I'll be fine. But I'll take a few painkillers, if you have them."

"If you're sure, man," the EMT said doubtfully as he wrapped my foot in an Ace bandage. By that time, crime scene techs were crawling all over the woods. An hour later Chavez came back from the bridge and gave me an update.

"The cars we have on the perimeter haven't found anything. I sent an officer down to the co-op to knock on doors and see who was and wasn't there. Most everyone was at home. Not that the person who did this didn't have time to get back to the co-op. But we'll go over everything in the morning. You should go and get some rest."

I didn't argue. I crawled into the van and drove back to the motel, thankful it was my left foot that was injured and that the van didn't have a stick shift.

Mauser met me at the door, almost as if he'd missed me. Though he was probably just looking for an opportunity to step on my injured foot, which he managed to do repeatedly. I took him for a quick, painful walk, then retreated to a hot shower.

Crawling into bed with ice on my foot, I called Cara and told her everything that had happened. She wanted to come over, but I told her truthfully that I needed to get some sleep. Next I texted Dad that I'd had a bit of trouble, but was fine. I wanted to make sure that if he heard anything through the sheriff's grapevine, I'd already told him the gist of it. At last I turned the light off and let the pain pills do their thing.

But by three o'clock I was wide awake, my mind churning over what had happened to Billy. Then something else occurred to me. Whoever was doing the killing might target Henry next. If they had planned on him being framed for the murders and those plans were thwarted, then they might decide to take direct action against him. I looked at my watch and decided I should wait until morning before going back to Cara's. There was no sense getting everyone upset over something that probably wasn't an issue.

I told myself that a dozen times. But my mind kept asking: *What if he's stalking Henry right now? What if the killer is trying to figure out a way to break into the house? To creep up the stairs? Maybe he'll kill everyone in the house. He certainly didn't hesitate to set me up for death or injury.*

Mauser moaned in irritation as I flipped and flopped in the bed, trying to get comfortable enough to forget my fears and go back to sleep. But my foot throbbed and every other muscle ached from the fall. And I couldn't stop thinking about Cara and Henry. At four I gave up and turned on the light. I got up, threw on some clothes and eased my bandaged foot into my hiking boot, stretching the laces as far as they would go. It was going to be a long day.

"Sorry about this, boy-o," I told Mauser. "But I might not be back in time to walk and feed you this morning, so you need to come with me." He groaned loudly as I put on his collar. "I can't wake your friend Mrs. Perkins at this time of night. Sorry." He stretched his legs out one more time before grudgingly getting to his feet.

Forty-five minutes later we were parked outside of Henry's house. I got out and made my way slowly and painfully around the house, making sure that nothing looked out of place, no windows broken or locks pried open. Satisfied, I figured I would keep watch from the van for the rest of the night.

A noise caused me to jump and open my eyes. It was

morning. My foot was aching and, even wrapped up in a quilt I'd taken from the motel room, I was freezing. Cara was staring through the window at me. I turned the key and rolled the window down. The rising sun burned my eyes.

"What are you doing out here?"

"I was worried the killer might be after your father," I told her, trying not to let her see how much pain I was in. Mauser chose that moment to roll over in the back of the van and give Cara a thunderous bark of greeting. "Yeah, thanks a whole lot for the early warning, you lazy dog." Cara smiled as Mauser got to his feet and stuck his head into the front of the van so she could pet him.

"Are you in a lot of pain? That's a stupid question, I can see you are. Let me walk Mauser and you go inside, get warm and have some breakfast."

It was almost seven-thirty when I made my way into the house. I found bananas, milk and cereal. I was on my second bowl as Henry came out of the bedroom.

"Good morning. You look awful," he said with brutal honesty. He went to the counter and began the most elaborate coffee-making process I'd ever seen. "It takes a few minutes, but I promise you that it'll warm you all the way down to your toes."

The smell of the brewing coffee started to revive me. Henry sat down across from me as I ate my cereal. He took one of the bananas and began to peel it, then stopped and looked me square in the eyes.

"I think you saved my life," he said in a somber tone. "I couldn't have stayed in jail another day."

"You'd have found the strength," I said, embarrassed.

"Maybe when I was younger. Now?" He shrugged. "I've spent most of my life outdoors and being caged in that crypt was too much."

"I know you didn't do anything wrong. It was just a matter of time until we got you out. You know, Lt. Chavez is a pretty good guy and a good investigator. I think he smelled something fishy from the start."

Henry seemed to think about this for a while. He got up and poured both of us a cup of coffee. Drinking the nutty dark brew made my whole body feel like I was standing in front of a warm fire.

"I'm glad Cara's seeing you." Henry waved his hand dismissively. "Not because of what you did for me, but because I think you're a good man. Everyone needs someone by their side." He drank half of his cup of coffee in one go.

"I wasn't sure if she *was* going to see me again."

"Cara told me that she had doubts. But when she told me why you were a deputy, I said that a man who stands by his family is the type of man you want." He finished the rest of his cup and set it down carefully on the wooden table. He was an interesting set of contrasts. Large and obviously strong, with a gentle manner. Quiet, but with a temper hidden deep within. I got the feeling there was a child hiding under that Viking exterior.

"I need to talk with folks around here again. I'm pretty sure that one of them is the killer," I told him.

"That's hard for me to believe."

"The three men who were killed were capable of doing some very bad things. I think they kicked a hornet's nest with someone around here. And the killer has proven he has it in for you too."

Henry looked up sharply, his eyes narrowing. "I guess you're right. But I don't know what I've ever done to anyone that they'd want to frame me for murder."

I was about to tell him that we'd figure it out when the door opened and Mauser came charging over to us. He bounced into me first and then Henry. The morning walk in the cool air had left him crazed. He continued to ricochet between Cara, Henry and me until Anna came out of the bedroom so he could include her in his high-speed game of bump-a-human. At last he settled down and dropped dramatically to the floor.

"I'll make him some breakfast," Cara said.

I looked around the room and, for just a flash, I got a vision of what it would be like to be with Cara, visiting her parents for Christmas. Of course, my dream world did not necessarily include a black-and-white elephant.

But the reality was that my whole body ached, my foot worst of all, and I still had a job to do. If I didn't find the person responsible, how could I go back to Adams County and leave Cara's family to fend for themselves?

CHAPTER NINETEEN

Anna convinced all of us to eat eggs fresh from their chickens and bacon from one of the hogs the co-op had butchered last month. I chased this with a couple pain pills left over from the night before and began to formulate a plan for the morning. I looked at Cara's map and decided on a few people to re-interview and some others that I hadn't had a chance to speak with yet.

Henry provided me with a walking stick that a neighbor had carved for him, which made my hobbling a little less painful. Cara offered to drive me around the co-op while Henry and Anna agreed to babysit Mauser, even after he managed to knock over a can of paint and wade through it before walking on one of Anna's paintings.

"No, really, I think he has something here," Anna said, looking at a couple of Mauser's five-inch-wide paw prints liberally spread across the beach landscape. "There are those elephants that paint. Seriously, his choice of colors is impressive." Mauser, tongue hanging out, wagged his tail and looked back and forth between us.

"Okay, great, just don't compliment his work too much. His ego is already tough enough to deal with."

I didn't know how many people would be willing to talk

to us on a Sunday morning, but Cara reiterated that everyone at the co-op was behind Henry. I didn't point out that at least one person wasn't. I think they were still finding it hard to believe that one of the co-op's members had a vendetta out on Henry. Of course, I could have been making too much of it. Maybe Henry was just a convenient scapegoat to frame for the first two murders. They *did* seem to abandon that pattern on the last killing.

I'd planned to start with the folks I hadn't had a chance to interview yet, but one of the previous interviews was still bugging me.

"I want to go back to Karen Gill's house," I told Cara. "She was hiding something from us. Before we go off doing a bunch of new interviews, I want to go back and see if we can cross her off the list or…" I shrugged.

"I'll give her a call."

I made my way gingerly onto Karen's porch as Cara rang the doorbell. Karen answered, wearing the same large smile. She greeted Cara as an old friend and nodded in my direction.

"Come in. Though I don't know what else I can tell you," she said, ushering us inside. A bright-eyed young girl sitting on the sofa looked up from the book that she was reading. "Andi, take your book and go to your bedroom."

"But…" the girl said, though she was already getting up off the couch.

"No buts. Go on."

The girl rolled her eyes at her mom and headed down a hallway.

Once her daughter had closed her bedroom door, Karen turned back to us. "Have a seat." She indicated the couch.

"Well, now, what can I do for you?" Her eyes were still bright and her smile firmly in place.

"When Lt. Chavez and I were here on Friday, we got the impression that you weren't telling us everything you knew," I said bluntly.

Her smile faltered just a bit. "I don't know what gave you

that impression."

"I think it was the fact that you were lying." I slammed the ball back into her court.

Karen looked at Cara, which I thought was odd. "No. I... Why would I lie?" she stuttered.

It was always nice to question someone who wasn't good at lying. "That's what I'm asking you. Why did you lie to us?"

Again she darted a glance at Cara before answering my question. "But I... didn't," she said lamely.

I'm a little slow, but I finally realized that if she was going to tell me the truth it wouldn't be in front of Cara.

"Let me be clear. You know that I'm from up near Tallahassee. I don't care about anything that's happening here except the murder. We can speak privately if you want, and everything that doesn't directly relate to the murder can be off the record," I said. I could see that she was thinking about it. "Permanently off the record."

Karen looked at Cara again, so I asked, "Cara, would you mind waiting outside?"

I could see that Cara's curiosity meter was going off the scale, but she got up and reluctantly left the house.

Karen looked close to crying. She turned away and stared out the window.

"You can trust me," I said and immediately thought it was probably the worst thing to say. But what else could I offer her? "What didn't you tell us last time?" I asked as compassionately as I could.

"You'll think... I guess it doesn't really matter. Okay. I knew Doug better than I said before," she said, turning to face me, then looking quickly at the floor.

"How much better?" I asked, having some idea where this was going.

"A lot. Well, I didn't really *know* him. I mean, I had sex with him."

"Voluntarily?"

"Voluntarily. Makes it sound like I was working for the Salvation Army. Willingly, ardently, and with abandon, yes.

He gave me a good once over the first time I went to his place, and one thing led to another. So sue me. I like to have sex. A lot. And he was pretty good in a *Looking for Mr. Goodbar* sort of way."

"Mr. Goodbar?"

"The movie? Guess you're too young. Woman goes looking for a wild time with men who are rough. Doug liked it rough and sometimes I do too. It was fun, a little naughty having sex with a guy you hardly know."

She was looking at me again, waiting for judgment. She'd be waiting for a long time. From a law enforcement point of view, people having fun, willing sex is a good thing. Keeps them happy and off the streets.

"And you didn't tell us this the first time…?"

"I know how some of the women feel about me. If they heard about this, it just wouldn't… It wouldn't help me any."

"How many times?"

"Three. The first time we met and then he came over a couple times after that."

"He initiated the encounters?"

She sighed, clearly embarrassed to be talking about it. "The first time it was mutual. We both saw the other wanted it and… Each time after that he seemed less interested. Finally…" She didn't go on.

"Finally what?"

"I went over there and tried to interest him one night. He seemed irritated that I came over and pretty much threw me out," she said, fighting through the humiliation of having to admit that in the end her advances were rejected.

"When was the last time?"

"The last time we actually… Or the time he didn't want to?"

"The time you went to him."

"The early part of October. I don't remember exactly what day."

I decided that there was no way to make her feel better

157

about having to admit her most intimate desires to a stranger, so getting out the door as soon as possible seemed the best course of action. I asked a couple more questions about the man and his behavior, but she didn't have anything else of note to tell me. I assured her that I'd keep this all quiet unless it somehow figured into the murder investigation.

Back in the van, I could tell that Cara wanted to ask me about Karen and I was impressed that she didn't. We agreed to move on to the new interviews. This was a true fishing expedition.

No one was home at the next house we tried, but we got lucky at the third. Cara introduced me to Milly and Cathy, two semi-retired college professors. Milly had taught English literature for thirty-five years and Cathy had been a civil engineer for twenty years before taking a teaching position. Both were dressed in sensible, comfortable Sunday lounging clothes.

"We heard about all that drama," Milly said, clearly fascinated and repelled at the same time. "Murder most foul." I pegged her for the type of person who slowed down and looked when passing an accident on the highway.

"It's not something to be made light of," Cathy said. "People have died."

"I knooooooow that. But life is about death, isn't it?" Milly said as though she was posing the question to class of sophomores.

"I don't think he's here for a philosophy lesson."

"Of course not, though I don't know what he thinks he can learn from us."

"I just want to ask some questions. It's best if you don't think about what I'm looking for. Just answer the questions the best you can."

"If we're trying to figure out what you want, that might skew our answers?" Cathy asked.

"Exactly. First, did you all know Timberlane?"

"I met him several times," Milly said. "Very odd duck.

The first time he gave me the once over, but I guess he didn't like what he saw. After that it was all business."

"Business?"

"When he had a question or needed something. They lived right through there." She pointed out a window. "This time of year with the leaves off the oaks, you can see the lights of the trailers at night. Cathy had more to do with him than I did."

I turned and looked at Cathy expectantly.

"With my experience in civil engineering, I get asked by the board to evaluate some of the little projects around here. Drainage issues, road problems, that sort of thing. Since Doug worked odd jobs for the co-op, we worked together a couple times."

"Anything odd happen when you were working with him?"

"Odd?" she asked herself. "Not really."

"Did he seem fixated on any women in the co-op?"

"He was a man. He didn't act much different than most of the guys I've seen on construction sites. He may have eyeballed someone, but honestly I don't remember. I've pretty much learned to ignore men's boorish behavior."

"What about Gibson? Did you all know him very well?"

"I met him several times. Not as creepy as Timberlane. I saw him at community dinners and he seemed just like some of the other damaged people we sometimes get staying here," Milly said.

"Damaged people?"

"Folks who have been abused in one way or another. People who ran away from abuse when they were young and are still trying to recover. It usually takes them time to trust. And their social skills aren't as practiced as people who have had a loving and nurturing upbringing."

"He grew some weed and used that to meet folks here. I think that most people here got along with Tommy, more so than Doug," Cathy allowed.

I held out my phone with a picture of Billy Good. "What

about this man? Did either of you ever see him around here?"

They both gave it a good hard look. Milly shook her head. "No, I don't think so."

Cathy nodded. "I did. It was strange now that I think about it. I got home one day after working with Doug on a drainage problem." She looked beyond me, clearly replaying the events in her mind. "When I was cleaning out the back of my truck I noticed that he'd left his tool belt there. I was kind of surprised that he hadn't called me since I'd left him at work about lunch time. I decided I'd walk it over to the trailers. There's a rough path that leads from the side of our place to the backyard of theirs. I walked through and saw Tommy, Doug and that fella," Cathy pointed to my phone, "standing around an old steel barrel. A fire was burning in the barrel, which was odd in and of itself since it was a warm day in October. You aren't allowed to burn household trash, but the odor coming from the fire in the barrel wasn't yard trash or wood. It was thick black smoke with a synthetic odor."

"What did they do when they saw you?"

"They looked at each other like guilty kids. Well, Tommy and that guy did. Doug stared at me like he was wondering what he should do or, maybe, could do, while the other guys looked at him."

"What happened?"

"Nothing. I held up his tool belt and told him I'd found it in the back of my truck. Doug said thanks and came over rather quickly and took it from me. Which surprised me a bit, since normally he was the type of arrogant guy who'd make me carry it over to him. But he seemed like he didn't want me to get a closer look at the fire barrel."

"Anything else?"

Cathy thought some more. "There was something hanging out of the barrel. A piece of cloth. The tail of a shirt, maybe? That's all I remember. After he took his belt, I turned around and came home."

"Did you ever see the third guy again?"

"No. That was the first and last time."

"Could you pinpoint when you saw them with the fire?"

"Sure, I keep a record of all the repairs we do. I should be able to go back and check my records."

"Believe me, she is meticulous," Milly laughed. Cathy nudged her good-naturedly and got up.

She returned a few minutes later. "October sixteenth."

We talked a bit more then Cara and I excused ourselves. Outside I said, "I want to go back to Mr. Riggs and ask a few more questions."

Our return to the oldest hippy in Florida gave us only a little more information. He was pretty sure that he could put the date when he saw the three men together sometime in the middle of October. Next I called Reed Holly, and he was able to give me a date in early October for their troubles with Timberlane.

I looked at my watch and saw it was nearly noon. "Let's head back to your folks. We shouldn't leave them with a hungry Mauser," I told Cara, which got a chuckle out of her.

"It was probably a great idea leaving Mauser with them. They needed something to take their minds off of all the crap that's been going on."

We enjoyed lunch with Anna and Henry. She'd made several vegetarian Tex-Mex dishes that were much better than they sounded. I made a point of not talking about work while we were eating and everyone seemed to be on board with that, but by the time we were eating homemade ice cream with muscadine sauce, Henry couldn't restrain himself.

"Have you found out anything?"

I looked around the table to see if I should go into detail and Cara gave me a nod, while her mother smiled and seemed interested.

"Maybe. I think around the fifteenth of October, Timberlane was working himself up to doing... something."

"Something?" Henry asked.

I was trying to be delicate, but that was silly considering everything that had happened. "I think he was a rapist at the least. If you hadn't caught him when you did, he would have done God knows what to Ellie Zacapa. Serial rapists and murderers often have cycles. Like the moon, but they can be over any length of time. It might be months or years, and often the cycle's time frame can change depending on what stressors the person is under."

"So they become more and more aggressive and dangerous as they reach their peak?" Cara asked.

"Exactly. And often after they've killed or raped, they'll go into a period of low activity. They might feel ashamed of their behavior, or at least feel like the pressure of the psychosis has been relieved for a time." I looked at Anna to make sure we weren't upsetting her. She met my eyes and seemed to read my thoughts.

"I can handle it. Maybe I haven't reacted very well," she reached out and took Henry's hand, "but this has been a shock. I *know* there is evil in the world. I've spent most of my life focusing on the good. I think evil is more like a disease than it is something people choose."

"I don't think that's how our killer sees it. Evil or not, Timberlane had rights. The person we're hunting has crossed a very distinct line. And if he's hunting you," I nodded toward Henry, "then he's gone from being a vigilante to a cold-blooded murderer."

"I wonder," Henry said very solemnly. "Maybe I *am* guilty. If Ellie had been harmed, I would have had to bear some of the responsibility for it."

"I don't see that," Cara said forcefully.

"I made the choice to let Timberlane live here. That's on me. Clearly I didn't do a good enough job checking him out. I got lazy."

"Henry, you're a good man. You can't distrust everyone who comes to our door," Anna comforted him.

I took a deep breath. There was information I still couldn't give them. I'd walked very close to the edge as it was. But I felt like a creep sitting there knowing how much better Henry would feel if he knew about Tyler's fake ID.

At one-thirty I decided to call Chavez, figuring he should be done with church by then, if he went. I was interested in what the preliminary reports on the Good killing said, plus I wanted to go over some of the other reports and records. Since I wasn't an Alachua County deputy, I couldn't exactly walk into the sheriff's office and start asking for stuff.

Chavez picked up on the second ring. "Larry, how are you feeling?" He sounded genuinely concerned.

"I'm hanging in there. I've been re-interviewing some of the witnesses. I didn't want to bother you on Sunday morning, but I need to get as much done as possible while I'm in town." I thought giving him the hope of getting rid of me some day might make my interference more tolerable.

"I understand. But you ought to rest. You really should have gone to the hospital last night."

"I'm fine. It's not the first time I've had a sprain. And it's not like they could have done much for it. Really, I'm feeling better already."

It was a crappy lie, but Chavez let it go. "Did you find out anything from the witnesses?"

"I've got an idea that I'd like to pursue."

"Care to share it with me?"

"I'd like to see some of the reports and some of your department's records. I know it's Sunday…"

"My wife has given up on me. I'll meet you at the station in forty-five minutes," he said and hung up.

I looked over at Cara. "Hey, Chauffeur. Want to drive me to the sheriff's office?" She rolled her eyes and gave me a little smile that made some of the pain go away.

CHAPTER TWENTY

Cara parked at the sheriff's office and waited in the van while I made my slow way up to the door. The duty officer paged Chavez, then I gave him a brief rundown of what I'd learned that morning.

"You're thinking something happened around October fifteenth that led to all of the murders?" He only sounded a little skeptical.

"I think he was reaching a fever pitch, and the events that people have described seem to indicate that was the case. Whatever he did, or *they* did, because I think the other two were involved in it, led to a revenge killing spree."

"Perhaps." He seemed to think about it. "That's not far off of our original theory, that Henry was appalled by Tyler's behavior toward Ellie and things escalated out of control from there." He held up his hand. "I realize that theory is outdated. Especially with the most recent killing, which Henry could not have been involved in."

"I want to look at the police reports and, maybe more importantly, your 911 call log to see if there is anything that jumps out."

"There are no reports from any of the houses in the co-op for the last six months. We ran all of the addresses before we did interviews so we could give the officers doing the interviews a heads-up. Nothing. And 911 calls on landlines are immediately linked to an address. So what you'd be looking at are just 911 calls from cell phones where the caller didn't leave a name or address."

I hadn't thought it all the way through, but Chavez had narrowed down the search very nicely. I often felt humbled when in the presence of a really good investigator.

I sat down with the list of cell phone calls. There were more than you would think. In the fourteen days surrounding October fifteenth there were forty cell phone hang-ups to the sheriff's office. They represented three different carriers, each of which would have to be presented with a request for information through formal channels. Of course, they could refuse and a warrant would be necessary. I didn't really want to wait weeks. I looked at the list. I could simply call all the numbers. It might work. The 911 operator would have done that at the time if the person had just hung up, but most of them were listed as misdialed calls. Only five were actual hang-ups.

"I'm going to call the hang-ups," I stated flatly. Chavez shrugged as if to say, *Knock yourself out.*

I took the sheet and dialed each number. Three didn't answer and their voicemails weren't set up. They were probably pay-as-you-go phones that someone had thrown away. The other two were answered by people who swore they didn't know who had called the sheriff's office. Both of them were willing to tell me who they were and where they lived. After they had done that, I went on to tell them not to give out their personal information to someone who calls up out of the blue and claims to be from the sheriff's office. My PSA for the day.

I took a deep breath and decided that it wouldn't be the biggest waste of my time to call the rest of the numbers on the list. I hated cold calls. I'd worked in a call center for about a week when I was in college. It was the only time I've ever been fired for being too nice.

I got through twenty-five calls, half of them unanswered, before I got a bingo.

"Hello?" said the voice on the other end. It was an older female.

"Hello, I'm Deputy Larry Macklin calling from the sheriff's office." I decided not to cloud the issue with *which* sheriff's office I was with. "The records show that you made a call to 911 at five-thirty on October fifteenth. According to the report, you called and said that there was someone outside, but then changed your mind, saying that it was probably nothing. You hung up after apologizing to the operator."

"I guess I… Oh, yes, I remember now. I thought I heard a noise outside in the woods. Shook me up for a moment. I'm really very sorry to have caused any trouble."

"If you could give me your name and where you live, that would be a big help."

"I guess you're really with the sheriff's office if you knew about the call." She had a point. "I live in the co-op just north of Gainesville."

I sat up so fast I bumped my injured foot against the desk and almost blurted out the f-bomb. "Where in the co-op?" She gave me an address that was on the east circle, putting it almost in the middle of the property. I told her a little bit about what I was working on and asked if I could come talk to her.

"Oh, of course. Horrible business."

I told her I'd be by around three o'clock. I would barely have time to look at some of the Good reports before I'd need to leave, but I didn't know how much longer I could stay away from Adams County. If nothing else, at some point I had to return Mauser to Dad. I'd texted him earlier and he was expecting to get home sometime around midnight. I updated him on everything and he told me to take a couple days to let my foot heal. He even said he'd drive down if necessary and pick up Mauser. The old man was a pain in the ass sometimes, but he was a good man.

I decided that I'd wait on the rest of the phone numbers. I was pretty sure that I had what I was looking for. I found Chavez at his desk, busy typing his reports on the Good murder. He looked up.

"You know, I still need to interview you about what happened last night."

I looked at my watch. I told him about the call and when I was supposed to meet the woman.

"I'll make it short," he said. "And don't worry about looking at the reports from last night. There's nothing there that will give you any new answers. I had some officers and a couple techs comb the site this morning, but it will be weeks before we get anything from the material they collected."

"Okay, let's do it."

After a relatively painless interview, Chavez walked me out to the van where Cara was reading something on her phone. She looked up and smiled. Chavez apologized for all the trouble that her family was going through and told me to call him if I learned anything.

"So you haven't met Ms. Kubelik yet." It was less a question than a statement. "You're in for a treat," Cara said with an odd smile.

Once in the co-op, we drove back to a small cottage. It was wood-framed with herbs hanging to dry on the front porch. I'd seen the house several times going through the neighborhood, but I didn't think I'd ever seen a car in the driveway.

As if anticipating my comment, Cara explained, "Ms. Kubelik doesn't drive. She either walks or relies on the kindness of strangers." She smiled. "Well, not strangers. Usually she shanghaies one of the co-op members into taking her to the store or wherever she wants to go."

The door opened as soon as we stepped up onto the wooden porch. The woman who stood there could have answered a casting call for a Brothers Grimm witch. She had a long narrow face framed by long black and grey hair. She wore gypsy jewelry and a multi-colored floor-length dress.

"Come in," she beckoned. Once we were inside she took Cara's hand in both of hers. "Cara, it is so nice to see you again." She looked at Cara's hand, turning it over and tracing the palm with her finger. "Yes, you're doing well. Good, good."

Then she turned her eyes to me and I felt as though I was being opened up and examined from the inside out. "I see," she said finally.

"I'm Deputy Macklin," I said lamely.

"You can call me Maria. You're in pain," she said, looking down at my leg. I tried to step back as she bent over and reached out to touch my calf. "Stand still, I won't hurt you."

I started to tell her to back off, but I guess I was in her witchy thrall. Her hand felt very warm, even through my pants leg. The heat traveled down to my foot and I swear the pain diminished. After a moment she straightened up.

"I'll fix you something."

"No, really, I'm fine."

"Of course you aren't. Just take a second," she said and left Cara and me standing in the living room while she went into the small kitchen. We could see her through the open doorway as she piddled about with ingredients.

Cara leaned in and whispered to me. "Mom comes to her for any aches and pains she has, but Dad is scared to death of her."

"You could have warned me," I whispered back. Cara gave me a wicked little smile.

In a few minutes Maria came back carrying a mug of something that smelled sweet with an odor of cinnamon, ginger and something else I couldn't quite put my finger on.

"Drink this," she said as she handed me the mug. "All of it now."

I thought about protesting, but I didn't want to get the interview off to a confrontational start. I looked at Cara for guidance and got raised eyebrows and that devilish grin. So down the hatch it went. It was warm, but not too hot and the warmth seemed to spread throughout my body.

"Let's sit down," Maria said, waving to a large round table in the middle of the living room. The ceiling was low and the house was decorated with all kinds of odd wall-hangings. We each took a seat around the table as though we were about to perform a séance.

"You want to know about my call to the sheriff's office," she stated as though she was doing a reading.

"Yes. What made you call?"

"I could say that it was a noise in the back woods. And that would be true. But it was more than the noise." Dramatically, she let that hang in the air. "I felt a great evil pass by my house."

"Could you describe the noise?" I didn't want to get too sidetracked by the evil feelings.

"The noise…" She looked up at the ceiling and closed her eyes. "It was part grunt and part scream, I'd say."

"A scream? And yet you didn't let the 911 operator send someone out?"

"You hear things that sound like screams out here in the woods. It could have been a screech owl, a bobcat or a housecat. The feeling is what made me call."

"But you didn't follow through?" I asked and this got me a narrow-eyed look from Maria.

"No, because I knew that I wouldn't be able to explain my feeling. I'm not stupid and I didn't need some smarty-pants policeman smiling behind my back. Besides, the feeling passed."

"Did you see or hear anything else that day? Before or after the noise?"

"Nothing unusual, I don't think. That was a couple of months ago. And I'm sure you know that people don't remember the routine things. If it was something that I saw all the time, particularly before I heard the noise, I wouldn't be likely to remember." She was right, and it left me with little to go on.

I couldn't think of anything else that might help. I felt a little discouraged and I was having a hard time letting it go. "Do you mind if we take a quick walk through the woods behind your house?"

Outside the air was pleasantly cool, one of those Florida winter days that are so beautiful it breaks your heart. The smell of oak wood burning in the distance added to the feeling of home and hearth. Cara and I looked around the back of the house until I found a deer path that lead in the direction of the rental trailers. I studied Cara's map for a moment.

"Your foot feeling better?" Cara asked.

"Actually it is," I said, somewhat startled. I hadn't realized that I was using the walking stick less.

Cara smiled, then pointed into the woods. "We're about halfway between Debbie and Reed Holly's house and the trailers. Terri Andrews's place is a little farther that way." With a lot of the oak trees having lost their leaves, I could just make out the Andrews place, but couldn't quite see the others.

"Let's spread out a bit and search from about fifty yards toward Timberlane's and fifty yards toward the Hollys'," I suggested.

"So you're thinking that Timberlane was going through the woods from his place to the Hollys'?"

"Exactly. Maybe he was still casing the place for a robbery, or maybe he was looking for an opportunity to do something worse. Maybe he *did* do something worse." Saying it out loud, I realized I was putting the Hollys in the center of the crosshairs. Maybe.

The fallen leaves made it difficult to see the trails. We separated and followed deer trails, looking for anything that might have been a clue to something we weren't even sure had happened. It was frustrating.

"I'm getting cold," I said, limping up to Cara, who thought she'd seen something that turned out to be a leaf.

The sun was setting and a chill breeze cut through the trees.

We made our way back to the van. I got in while Cara went to tell Maria that we were done. I decided that if she had heard something, then maybe Terri had. The last time that I'd talked with her, I didn't have a timeline. Now maybe I could give her more to go on. I pulled out my phone. I almost dialed and thought better of it. It was almost six here so it would be almost midnight in Rome. Better to wait. I put the phone down as Cara got into the van.

"When did the Andrewses get here?" I asked her.

"Hard to say. Sometime in October. We can ask Dad."

"We need to go back to take Mauser for a walk and feed him anyway."

Cara started the van and we wound our way over the dirt roads. Colorful lights on many of the homes reminded me that it was only a couple weeks until Christmas.

Mauser jumped up and gave a big bellowing bark when we came in. Henry was sitting at the table working on a piece of wood with a Dremel tool. He put the tool down quickly as Mauser came bouncing past him on the way to greet us.

"He's already bumped my arm about a dozen times," Henry said in mock irritation while Mauser bounced between Cara and me.

"We thought he might be ready for a walk and some dinner," I said.

"He shouldn't be that hungry since he got a fresh baked loaf of bread off the counter."

"He didn't," Cara said in a good-humored voice while scratching Mauser vigorously.

"You get away with things that no other dog would," I told him. He looked up at me, tongue hanging out as though he knew exactly what I was saying and couldn't care less.

Luckily for us, Anna had baked two loaves, so we were able to have fresh bread with warm homemade barley soup that had been on the stove for hours. I'd almost settled into this Hallmark-card evening, but something kept nagging at me. Henry eyed me from across the table.

"You still thinking about the murders?"

"Can't really get them out of my head."

"Are you leaving us tomorrow?"

"No, I've arranged to stay another day."

"I called Dr. Barnhill and asked for two more days off too. He didn't seem to mind too much. I think he likes having Alvin around. He's been taking him home at night," Cara said. She'd confided to me that even Barnhill had his limits and that she'd have to head home in two days, regardless of the status of the case.

Of course, finding the killer was only the first part of the battle. There'd still be a lot more work to do, and ultimately a trial. But identifying the suspect was the first and most vital step on the way to the wrapping this up and letting Cara's family go back to living their lives in peace.

"Thank you both for being here," Henry said, reaching his hands out to both Cara and Anna.

"I still can't see how anyone who lives here could have done anything like that," Anna said.

"Someone targeted those three men and you. I think you have to accept that the killer is someone you know," I said. "Let's go back to the phone calls you received. Think about the voice. Could you have recognized it?"

He closed his eyes. "He might have been purposely disguising his voice. It's possible that it was someone I know." He shrugged.

"Think about means, motive and opportunity," I said. "I don't feel like we've found out much about any of them. Means? Doesn't require much. Rope and probably a gun. No great physical strength. We can eliminate men over eighty years old, probably, and Mr. Andrews, who is too physically impaired, but not many other people. Opportunity? We've eliminated several people. Chavez's men checked out the alibis for Timberlane's murder and verified Riggs's and Holly's. But beyond that it's only two and a half hours to Adams County. The murderer spent part of the day casing Timberlane's place. I hate to put this on you, Henry, but they might have even followed you to Timberlane's. Opportunity doesn't rule out many people. Motive still has to be our focus."

"You think that the three of them raped or killed someone?" Cara said.

"I do. Then the question becomes who? The sheriff's office has two reports of females who went missing around mid-October. One turned up a few days later and the other one hasn't turned up, but has no connection to the co-op."

"Maybe it doesn't have anything to do with the co-op. Couldn't it have been a girl who lives in some other part of Gainesville? And the husband or boyfriend is someone we don't know?" Anna asked hopefully.

"Maybe they have an accomplice on the inside," Cara said.

"Someone from the outside with a friend on the inside? Not a bad idea. That would explain a few things. We have more females who might have been victims and very few males that could be our killer. But if a woman is passing information to someone who doesn't live in the community… I guess that's a possibility. Which gets us back to trying to discover the trigger event."

"Which you think happened around October fifteenth," Henry said.

"Yes. I think that Timberlane was working himself up to commit a rape, possibly a murder, a pattern we see with serial rapists and murderers. The incident with the Hollys, being warned off of Terri Andrews, grabbing Ellie." I stopped myself before mentioning that Tyler had also become dissatisfied with consensual sex with Karen Gill. "All of those events indicate that Timberlane was either building toward or in the throes of a sexual rage. Finally, I think that Cathy witnessed the three of them burning the clothes they wore when the act was committed."

"But who was the victim?" Cara asked

"It went unreported. All the rapes that Chavez and I found during that period already had suspects, or their related witness accounts eliminated our three—um, it's hard to know what to call them—they're victims and suspects both. An unreported rape is most likely. A rape that is being avenged by a boyfriend or family member. Someone who also blames you," I said, looking at Henry.

"I blame myself for all of this," Henry said. Anna put her hand on Henry's. "I know it's not really my fault, but I think I understand why someone feels that it is."

"I know that being raped would be devastating. A horrible trauma, but would someone really kill three people because they raped someone they loved?" Cara asked.

Henry and I answered at the same time. "Yes." Everyone around the table was quiet for a moment.

"So where do we go from here?" Henry asked.

"Re-interviewing folks with a focus on October fifteenth. We have to hope that someone will remember seeing or hearing something else. I'm going to call Chavez in the morning and have his crime scene techs go over Gibson's and Good's vehicles again with the thought that they might have been used for the rape or murder of someone else. I'll call our people and have Timberlane's truck gone over again too."

We talked for a little longer, but everyone was tired. My body was aching from the day before and my foot was beginning to throb. Maria's magic elixir was definitely wearing off. We packed Mauser into the van and headed back to the motel. I wanted to drive myself, but Cara insisted that I give it another day. On the way, I called my neighbor who was cat-sitting Ivy and she assured me that while Ivy wasn't happy, she was fine.

Cara got Mauser out of the van and walked him while I made my way into the room.

"What time do you want me to pick you up?" Cara asked as she helped me take my jacket off.

"Eight."

"You'll be all right with the big guy?" She nodded toward Mauser, who'd already jumped on the bed and monopolized all the covers.

"We'll manage."

She leaned in and we kissed. "I don't know how we would have gotten through this without you," she said.

"We aren't through it yet," I reminded her.

CHAPTER TWENTY-ONE

Cara had Mauser and me back at the co-op before nine. Anna insisted on serving us breakfast while we discussed the plan of attack for the day.

"Where do we start?" Cara asked brightly.

"I've been thinking. I want to go back and talk with Ms. Kubelik. Maybe she'll remember something else."

"Ha! You don't fool me. You just want to get more of that tea she made for you," Cara said, smiling.

"You know, it really did make my foot feel better," I acknowledged. "But I *do* want to talk to her."

Anna, who was working on a project in the living room, had overheard us. "I don't know why anyone would go to a doctor. Maria can work wonders."

"Okay, Maria first," Cara said, looking back at Mauser, who had settled comfortably on the living room couch. He'd be good until lunch.

Again, Maria managed to open the door before we got to it. Creepy.

"I thought you all would be back," she said, opening the door wide. I couldn't help thinking about Hansel and Gretel. "I'll make you some more herbal tea for your aches and pains. Go ahead and have a seat. I'll be back in a tic."

With my tea in hand and, yes, feeling better, I proceeded to ask her about the day she called 911.

"Have you been able to remember anything else about that day? Anything that was out of the ordinary."

"I have," she said without expanding on it.

"What?"

"Terri Andrews." Again without elaborating. Maria was clearly enjoying her dramatic moment.

"You saw her that day?" I asked.

"No."

"So you didn't see her?"

"Right."

"So?"

"I didn't see her the next day either," she stated with a *there you go* look on her face.

"I don't think I quite see your point," I admitted.

"Ah, but you see, I had seen her fairly regularly up until then."

"She came by often?"

"Terri went on jogs or runs, whatever she called them, almost daily. Most of the time she circled through the co-op before or after going out on the road. About every other day she'd stop in when she got done for a cup of tea. Sometimes she'd buy some of the liniment I made. It's really good for the muscles."

"But she stopped coming by?"

"Yes. I can't remember exactly when the last time was, but I'm sure that she didn't come by after that day."

"Of course, Terri went to Rome. And it was right around that time," Cara said.

"Funny about that too." Again Maria seemed to want us to drag it out of her.

"What's odd about it?" I asked.

"Like I said, about every other day we'd sit and have tea. We'd talk about a lot of things. But most of all she talked about her art. Never once did she say she was going to Rome. I don't even recall her saying that she wanted to go to overseas to study. Then, poof, she's gone. Very odd now that I think about it."

I had to admit that she might have been onto something. Could Terri have been attacked? Did she have a boyfriend who was avenging her honor? We stayed for a little longer, but I was anxious to follow up with Terri's parents.

Cara called them to make sure that they weren't at the hospital or scheduled for an appointment. "Larry, Deputy Macklin, has a few follow-up questions he wants to ask you," I heard Cara say. "Mostly about Terri, actually." Another pause. "My dad? Sure, I don't think he'll mind. I'll call him." Pause. "No problem, we'll be over in a little bit."

She disconnected the call and turned to me. "Mrs. Andrews said it's not a problem. Bill's having some problems with his wheelchair and she wanted me to ask Dad if he could come over and check it out. I'll give him a call."

"Don't bother. Let's just go straight to your dad's house. We can check on Mauser and take your dad with us. Might help having him as a distraction. He can occupy Bill while we talk to Amy and vice versa."

Henry was more than glad for something to do. He grabbed his tool box and followed us out to the van.

Amy Andrews threw open the door for us when we arrived. "Cara, good to see you again. Henry, I'm Amy, I know we met a couple of times when Bill and I moved in. Bill is in the back room. Would you mind taking a look at his chair?" She pointed Henry toward a bedroom and waved Cara and me toward the kitchen table. "We can sit in here and talk if you like."

Cara and I sat at the table and Amy offered us both a drink, which we accepted after she insisted. After bringing us both water, she took a chair across the table from us.

"Now, what did you want to ask us about?" she asked, smiling pleasantly.

"When did Terri decide to go to Rome?" I asked, thinking I'd start off with something easy.

"Well, I don't know exactly. Art has always been her life.

And, of course, Italy is the art capital of the world, right? I think she's always planned on going to Italy."

"I mean this trip specifically."

"Oh, months, I'm sure. She told us about it at the last minute, but with the accident it just all worked out that we could stay here."

"This was around the middle of October? You were on your way here when the accident occurred, right?"

"Yes, we were coming to visit Terri. It was the sixteenth of October. I won't ever forget that date." Her smile faltered as she thought about the accident that had left her husband crippled. Yet there was something else in her face. Anger.

I'm slow, but it was coming together in my mind. A cold chill ran down my spine when I realized where this was going.

"Something happened to Terri?" I asked, already knowing the answer.

"Why would you say that?" Amy tried to laugh it off, but her eyes were no longer smiling.

"That's why you were coming here. She called you and told you that she had been raped, so you and Bill jumped in your car. You were coming to your daughter's rescue. Hurrying, driving too fast. At night?" I asked, staring straight into Amy's eyes. Eyes that were now as cold and hard as steel.

"Aren't you the smart one? Yes, it was at night. You don't stop and sleep when you get a call from your daughter telling you that she's been brutally raped. Three hundred and fifty miles from Montgomery to Gainesville. She called us at ten o'clock. Crying, sobbing. I got her to tell us what had happened. By the time we were on the road, Bill was shaking with fear for Terri's safety and fury at the animals that did this. I don't think he could hear or see anything that night except the voice in his head that told him to hurry. To get to her, to protect her and to avenge her.

"I tried to reason with him and get him to drive carefully.

But he was a man possessed. A slick patch. That's what the highway patrol said. We hit a slick patch. The car spun and hit a tree. Bill's legs were crushed in the wreckage." Tears were running down Amy's cheeks. "He was life-flighted to Shands. Poor Terri, still in pain, had to meet us at the hospital. They saved Bill, but they couldn't save his legs."

Amy raised her left hand to wipe her cheeks, but she kept the right one under the table. "I stood by my husband as he came to terms with the fact that he would be a cripple for the rest of his life. And listened to my daughter recount the horrid, vile attack by those sub-humans that raped and defiled her."

"So you killed them."

Amy pulled her right hand out from under the table. In it she held a Beretta 92 handgun. "Of course I did," she said. Her eyes were on me and the gun was steady.

My hands were on the table, almost touching my full glass of ice water. Without dropping Amy's gaze, I reached out and tipped the glass over.

It is almost impossible for a person not to react when a glass is spilled and, sure enough, Amy jumped back. As soon as she moved and I was sure that the gun was not pointing at Cara or me, I shoved the table as hard and fast as I could at Amy, sending her flying backwards. She slammed into the floor with a scream. I limped over to her as quickly as I could and managed to stomp my good foot down on her hand. She released the gun and I bent down to grab it, pointing it at her as she stood.

"Stop right there." I could have drawn my own gun on her instead of taking the risk to disarm her, but if she had kept the Beretta I might have had to shoot her. And the truth was, killer though she might have been, I felt sorry for her.

"Are you all right?" I asked Cara, who looked stunned.

"Yes." She checked herself. "Yes, I'm fine." I saw her look behind me and her eyes got big. A cold hand clutched my heart. I hadn't thought about Bill and Henry.

"You can drop your gun now." I heard Bill's voice from behind me.

"Bill, don't forget he has his own gun too," Amy said helpfully.

"Turn around," Bill told me. I turned slowly to face a rather odd sight. Bill was sitting in his chair with a box on his lap, Henry standing next to him handcuffed to the chair.

"He has a bomb," Henry said, his voice shocked.

I looked closer at the box on Bill's lap. It was a simple bomb with a thumb-press ignition and four stick fuses.

"C-4. Amy and I were both in the military. Didn't know that, did you? That's 'cause you're crap at your job. Why the hell wouldn't you do a full background check on everyone here?" Bill asked, spitting the words out.

"Okay, I'm a shitty investigator. Fine. Now what?" I asked, figuring a show of strength was better than one of weakness with these two. They were both quickly losing my sympathy vote.

"First, put down the gun you're holding, slowly, and then take your gun out of its holster and put it on the ground," Bill answered.

"You can't get out of this," I said, slowly doing as he said and placing both guns on the floor.

"Who said I wanted out? Look at me. I'm a broken man." His voice was forged in anger. A man with nothing left to lose was a dangerous man indeed.

"What will killing us solve?" My second hostage crisis in two months; you'd think after the first one I would have read up on the subject, but who the hell would have thought it would happen to me again so soon?

"We've fixed most of the problem already. Honestly, I never saw myself surviving. Now my plan is simple. Just blow us up and call it a day." He tapped the bomb. Poor Henry was trying to stretch as far away from the bomb as he could get.

"I don't understand that. Why kill Henry?"

"Don't be so stupid! You know why. He let those people

move in here without vetting them. I've talked to the folks around here. Henry's the man who decides who can live here and who can't. Terri trusted this den of hippies. Always telling us how nice everyone was. Who was the guardian of the hen house? Him!"

He jerked the end of the handcuff attached to the wheelchair and looked at Henry. "You may as well come over here and cuddle up with this bomb. There's enough C-4 here to level the house and leave a crater ten feet deep. A foot or two isn't going to help you."

"Henry isn't to blame. He didn't know that Timberlane was an alias. Timberlane's real name was David Tyler, but he had a pretty good fake driver's license. Henry checked him out, but he was checking under an alias, not his real name."

"That doesn't matter. He still heard that Timberlane, whatever his name was, was harassing women and he didn't kick him out. Not until it was too late," Bill growled.

"Amy did the dirty work and you made the phone calls," I said, trying to keep the conversation going while I thought of a way to get us out of this mess. Turning to Amy, I said, "You tortured Tyler before you killed him."

"I liked taking the chair away and putting it back. It got him to talk. And what he went through was nothing compared to what they did to Terri," she spat back at me.

"We had to find out who all was involved," Bill said, adding wickedly, "That's the chair we used, right over there." He pointed to a straight-backed Shaker-style chair in the corner. "It was my grandfather's," he said proudly.

Bill was sweating profusely. He didn't look good at all. If he started to have a heart attack, would he just detonate the bomb? Who the hell knew? But it probably wasn't worth the chance.

"You don't look so good. Maybe Amy could bring you some water."

"Maybe you could shut up," he said, breathing heavily.

"Bill, he's right," Amy said, going to the sink and filling two glasses. On her way to her husband she stopped and looked me in the face before throwing the contents of one of the glasses at me. "That's for the water trick, asshole." She was definitely off of my sympathy list now.

Amy handed Bill the other glass of water and took a towel that was on the arm of the wheelchair and mopped his brow. "You look awful. How do you feel?"

He smiled up at her. "Love, I'm going to blow the shit out of myself and this asshole. It hardly matters how I'm feeling." He laughed. "Maybe it's better if I feel like crap."

Amy picked up the guns, putting my Glock on the counter and keeping the Beretta. "You don't really want to kill anyone else," I said, though even I didn't believe it.

"You're full of crap. I'm going to send my wife outside and then we're all going to get ripped into very small pieces." He indicated the explosive in his lap. "The only one left to explain what happened will be Amy."

After everything they'd done, that wasn't the worst plan. Not great, and it left a lot of loose ends for her to explain, but what else could they do?

"Is Terri going to believe whatever story Amy makes up? Or is she in on it too?" From the look on Bill's face I thought I might have pushed him right off the cliff into heart attack valley.

"Don't you dare talk about Terri! I've put up with enough of your bullshit. Amy, do you think you could explain away a bullet in this asshole? If you do, shoot him."

She pointed her gun at me and seemed to think about it. "He's not worth the bullet," she said.

"Where'd you get the C-4 explosive?" I was trying to sound cool, but the truth was I was close to peeing my pants. I'd choose a bullet over a bomb any day. The thought of being blown to smithereens gave me rubber legs. And I really didn't see a way out of this. I'd done my one parlor trick with the glass of water. I was twenty feet from a very determined suicidal man with a bomb and I had zero chance of getting to him before he had a chance to detonate it. Talking was all I could do, so I talked.

"I worked in ordinance when I was a captain. One day I was logging in a shipment and realized that there was an undercount. You'd be surprised at how much stuff walks off a military base. I took it just for the hell of it. That was about a year before McVeigh blew up the Morrow Building. After terrorism got to be the watch word, I didn't know how to get rid of it without getting into trouble. And if I threw it away, there was a chance that it would fall into the hands of a child or a bad person. Joke's on me, I guess. I'm the bad person."

"We can find a way out of this. Just give us a chance."

"Bullshit. Amy, get out of here," Bill said. He watched her leave and didn't see Henry shift back toward the wheelchair.

What I saw next helps to explain why other warriors were terrified of the Vikings. Pushed into a corner, they would do things that no sane man would even consider. With Bill momentarily focused on Amy's exit, Henry reached over and snatched the wires and fuses out of the homemade bomb. He did it so fast that by the time Bill tried to press the button, it wasn't attached to anything. And if that wasn't shocking enough, Henry then crammed the wires and fuses into his large mouth and swallowed them. The fuses were about half the length of a pen and smaller in diameter. I know that men have swallowed more and bigger things, but it was still impressive.

When Bill realized what had happened, he screamed and grabbed at Henry, who pulled away as best he could with his arm still handcuffed to the wheelchair. The chair tipped over, throwing Bill out onto the floor.

Amy came rushing back into the room, screaming at Henry. In her adrenaline-fueled tunnel vision, she forgot about me. I reached out for her as she passed me. But she realized her mistake just in time, turning away before I could get to her on my bum foot. Then something flew over my head and smashed into Amy's face. She stumbled back, dropping the gun and falling to the ground. Cara had hurled a chair at Amy. I was impressed.

I grabbed the Beretta as Cara went over to help her father escape the clutches of Bill, who was tearing at Henry with tooth and nail. Finally she had to just sit on the enraged man while Henry tried to recover and I held the gun on Amy. I pulled out my cell phone and called 911, giving them a CliffsNotes version of what had happened. Then I called Chavez.

"Playing cowboy," he joked once he knew we were all okay.

"I figured that was the only way a case would to get solved down here in gator country," I answered back, feeling giddy now that everyone was safe.

CHAPTER TWENTY-TWO

Hordes of deputies, the bomb squad and crime scene techs showed up and swarmed the house. Henry became an object of fascination, with everyone wanting to see the man that ate a bomb. As he was cut away from the wheelchair and loaded up for a trip to the hospital for X-rays, Henry kept reminding everyone that he'd only eaten the wiring. But it was still impressive.

"Why'd you eat it?" I asked.

"That was the only way I knew to be sure that it couldn't be used. I thought about just ripping it out and throwing it away, but what if he got it again? Or that crazy woman."

"If I hadn't been able to stop Amy, she might have tried to cut you open to get the wires back."

With a straight face he said, "That's why I chewed the wires before I swallowed."

I gave him a small salute as the ambulance pulled away. Nope, wouldn't want to fight Vikings.

Cara was sitting on the porch steps while techs and deputies came and went around her. I limped over and offered her my hand, pulling her to her feet and into a big hug.

"Thanks for the chair," I said.

"Anytime. Of course, for all you know, I was aiming for your head."

"The thought occurred to me." I got serious. "I hope this hasn't caused you to consider putting us on hold again." I knew it wasn't the right time to bring the subject up, but I couldn't help myself. After all that had happened, our relationship was still foremost in my mind. I was probably crazy.

Cara smiled. "No. I probably should. But I was serious. Life is about living and living is about risk. And this," she gestured to all the first responders, "was more about my family than your job. If you're willing to ride things out with me for a while, I'll give it a go." I hugged her more tightly.

"Come on. I should go tell Mom what happened," she said. We started toward the van, but then she stopped. "It isn't always like this, is it?" She sounded half serious.

"Oh, yeah, crazy women with guns and guys in wheelchairs with bombs. A normal week for me," I said and bumped her jovially.

I checked in with Chavez and got permission for Cara and me to leave the scene. We spent an hour giving her mother all of the details while she sat staring at us, her mouth hanging open. I couldn't blame her.

We took Mauser for a quick walk then left him napping on the Laursens' couch. Cara and her mom set off for the hospital to check on Henry and I left for the sheriff's office to hunt up Chavez. I still needed to wrap up my case. It was going to take a lot of team effort to sort it all out, deciding how to share the evidence and who had the primary responsibility for prosecuting the Andrewses.

I found Chavez at his desk, coat off and leaning back in his chair, reading reports. He stood up when he saw me.

"Macklin, is your life always this interesting? If so, I think you need to go back up north. Gainesville has enough crazy," he said with a big smile. "Seriously, it has been an honor. I guess we're both proof that your father is a very good teacher."

"I appreciate all your help, and I know that Cara and her family do too." I shook his hand. "What are you going to do about Terri Andrews?"

"I talked to the prosecutor. The most we could charge her with is prior knowledge and there isn't much cause for that. We agreed that pressing charges would just be cruel."

We flipped a coin to see who had to make the depressing phone call. I lost. Terri cried and cried some more. She really was in Italy. She said she hadn't wanted to leave her parents, but they had insisted. I told her that there was no need to hurry back. Her parents had already retained counsel so there wasn't much that she could do for them. It would probably be at least a year before they went to trial and bail was unlikely. Judges don't feel lenient when it comes to bomb-makers.

I called Dad and told him I'd be home the next day. I needed to get Mauser back to his home, and there was no point in me waiting around Gainesville any longer. It would take months before all the terabytes of forensic data were compiled and the reports written. Now that the killers were off the street, there wasn't any urgency in processing the evidence. The reports would arrive when they arrived.

I fetched Mauser from the Laursens' and went back to the motel. My foot, and most of the rest of me, was aching. I filled the tub with hot water and Epsom salts and soaked for an hour. When I got out there was a message on my phone from Cara: *Dinner?*

I answered: *Sure. Where?*

Her: *There? Comfort food—pizza?*

Me: *Perfect.*

Her: *I'll bring it. One hour.*

After dinner, we made love. It was slow and exploratory as we learned each other's bodies. Working around my injuries, we found our rhythm. Satisfied at last, we lay beside each other and held hands. We didn't speak much. For my part, I didn't want to take the chance of spoiling the moment. After a few minutes, Cara rolled over and slept. I fell asleep with the warmth and comfort of her body next to mine.

At some point during the night Mauser, the lumbering oaf, climbed into bed. I was much relieved in the morning to discover that the horrible snoring I heard coming from the other side of the bed was the dog and not Cara.

"Are you awake?" Cara asked.

"How could anyone sleep through that?" I asked, waving a hand in the direction of the canine buzz saw. I looked at my watch.

"Probably time to get up anyway," I said. We got the monster out of the bed, walked and fed. We still didn't talk much about the night before.

"I need to go to the hospital and see how Dad's doing," Cara said after getting cleaned up and dressed. "As long as the doctors say he'll be okay, I'm going back home today."

I held up my phone. "Let me know what you're doing?"

"You too," she said and leaned in for a kiss. She scratched Mauser, who'd gone back to bed. "You take care of him," she told the dog.

Mrs. Perkins came out to say goodbye and gave me a huge bag of goodies for Mauser, and then proceeded to scratch, pet and hug the big goofball while telling him what a great dog he was and how much she'd miss him. At last I managed to pry him loose from her clutches and get him situated in the back of the van.

Soon I was up on I-75 headed back to Adams County. The drive gave me time to think about all the complications with Matt that were waiting for me back home. How was I going to deal with the possibility that he was working for drug dealers? I decided I couldn't deal with it on my own.

My first order of business was to take my overgrown traveling companion back to where he belonged. Dad was standing on the porch when we drove up. He spent half an hour greeting Mauser, who seemed equally enthused to see him and to be home. I got a handshake.

"When you moved to criminal investigations, I didn't think you'd be putting yourself in harm's way every chance you got. You know, most deputies consider CID a desk job," he joked. "You want to come in out of the cold?"

Sitting across from Dad, I told him about the information I'd received from Eddie, how I'd staked out the industrial park, and the realization that I'd seen Matt's car. I was surprised when I didn't get any flack about going out on my own.

"There could be other explanations for why Matt was there." Dad slipped into sheriff mode, calm and judicious.

"I thought of that, but all the other explanations seem like a stretch. I think what really makes me wonder is his attitude change over the last month. He used to seem resentful most of the time. Now it's more like he knows something we don't, and it's making him smug."

"Regardless, all you have right now is a suspicion. His change in attitude could be related to something in his personal life. Without evidence, the only thing we can do is to keep a closer eye on him. Bring me something more concrete and we'll have a way forward," he said somberly.

"I feel better for having told you," I said sincerely.

"I'm not sure that I do. I have to treat him fairly and not hold unsubstantiated claims against him. Pretending like you know something when you don't is one thing. Acting as though you don't know something when you do is another. Of course, I *don't* know anything and that's the point. Neither do you."

"I get it," I said. Getting back on my feet took some effort. Mauser didn't even raise his head from the huge bed that Dad kept for him in the living room. "I don't get a thank you for your action-packed vacation?" Mauser refused to even open an eye.

I stopped by the office before heading home. I couldn't

help but look around for Matt's car. I didn't see it.

Pete was eating Christmas cookies at his desk near mine when I walked in. The big guy jumped up and gave me a hug. "Damn, I'm tired of doing your work," he said, patting my shoulder. "At least you managed to solve a homicide while you were on vacation," he joked and then pointed to a stack of reports on his desk. "Twenty cases I've covered while you were gone. Tomorrow it's lunch at Winston's Grill, and you're buying."

"Would it make you feel better if I told you I almost got blown up by a wheelchair bomb?"

He looked thoughtful for a moment. "No. I'm still ordering something expensive off the menu. And the gimpy leg routine isn't going to get you any sympathy either."

"I was only gone for three working days."

"Talk to the hand," he said as he grabbed another cookie and put on his coat. "Oh, the lieutenant wanted to see you when you got in. I've got to run out and talk to a witness on an assault charge—actually, multiple assault charges. Another great case that you missed out on. A fight broke out at a neighborhood Christmas party. Five people in the hospital. Two of them knifed. God bless us, everyone," he said as he went out the door.

I headed for Lt. Johnson's office and walked in when he acknowledged my knock. He sat straight-backed in his chair. I always felt like I should salute when I saw him. The man had spent almost twenty years in the Army's military police and had never really left it. I was sure that without his dark brown skin tone, his face would have spent most of its time glowing an angry red at all the non-military behavior around the station. This afternoon I got a tight-lipped smile from him.

"Congratulations on solving the Tyler homicide. But I do wish that you and the sheriff would at least acknowledge that I'm in the chain of command."

As soon as he said this, my mind went to Matt. What would the lieutenant say if he knew that we were keeping information on a potential bad cop from him? If it came to that, I'd have to let Dad deal with the fallout.

"From now on, at least copy me on texts and emails. Just in case I'm called on to make a decision involving one of your extracurricular activities," he said with a considerable amount of sarcasm. "You can count on getting a little extra work thrown your way since some of the other officers have been having to do double-duty while you were off solving Alachua County's cases."

Hey, one of those murders was ours, I thought, but decided it was better to keep that to myself.

"Go on, get out of here."

I had two other tasks on my to-do list before heading home. First I called Tammy Page, David Tyler's mother. I thought she deserved to hear what had happened from me before news stories and rumors started to circulate.

After leaving the office, I stopped and bought a six-pack of beer then drove out to Jeremy Wright's house. The old man wasn't on the porch, which gave me a bad moment, but a knock on the door brought a shout from inside.

"You had me worried when I didn't see you on the porch," I kidded him when he answered the door.

"Hell, I gotta pee sometime," he said with a smile that grew larger when he saw the beer. "Wahoo! Wait, I got something to go with it." He disappeared back inside the trailer and came out a moment later with a couple bags of boiled peanuts.

We sat on the porch and I drank a beer, ate peanuts and watched the sun go down as he told me about the jobs he'd had and the women he'd known. It was very relaxing.

I received a cold shoulder from Ivy when I got home. It took her an hour before she decided to forgive me for leaving her in the care of a neighbor, but finally she crawled into my lap as I talked to Cara on the phone. Henry had been told he'd live, but not to eat any more C-4 fuses. We set a date for dinner the next night.

I sat on the couch, petting Ivy and listening to the petite tabby purr, glad to be home. But I couldn't help thinking that, for all the trouble that was in the rearview mirror, there was a whole lot more coming down the road.

Larry Macklin returns in:

January's Betrayal
A Larry Macklin Mystery–Book 3

Here's a preview:

It was after midnight and cold. The first thing I saw when I pulled up behind the shopping center didn't make me feel better. Held back by crime scene tape were two news vans and my dad's pickup truck. As an investigator, the last things you want at your crime scene are reporters and the sheriff. And when the sheriff is also your father, you're doubly screwed.

On the other side of the tape, two of our patrol cars were parked at odd angles, all their lights on and illuminating the bodies of a man and a woman. As I parked my unmarked car, the crime scene van pulled up next to me. Shantel Williams and Marcus Brown, two of our best techs, got out and greeted me.

"None of this is good," Shantel said, carrying her box of equipment.

"I was told Nichols shot a suspect?"

"Not the half of it. He shot Ayers."

"Jeffrey Ayers, the suspect in the rapes?"

"That's what Marti in dispatch said," Marcus responded.

As we approached the scene, I could see my father staring at the bodies from a distance. He heard us coming and held up the crime scene tape so that Marcus and Shantel could go under. They set their boxes down and started removing their cameras.

Dad pulled me aside. Behind him, the news crews were already testing their lights and microphones.

"This is going to go political fast," he said, his voice low and ominous.

"What the hell happened?"

"That's what we're going to have to figure out. Look, I know you're on call tonight, but I'm going to need to assign another investigator as the lead."

"Because of Ayers?"

Jeffrey Ayers had been our chief suspect in a series of rapes. But as we dug deeper, the evidence pointed away from him and two days ago Dad had announced that Ayers was no longer considered a suspect.

Dad nodded to the news vans. "Press is already on top of the story. I have to be above this. If Ayers raped and killed this woman then I'm in big trouble. It's not going to help if it looks like I put my son in charge of the investigation. Perception is going to be almost as important as the reality."

"I understand."

"That doesn't mean I don't want you involved. This coming on the heels of what you told me about Matt..." He shrugged. "I'm not feeling very comfortable. You know Matt would have been my second choice."

Dad seemed to have aged ten years in the last month. Before Christmas I'd stumbled upon a situation suggesting that Matt Greene, one of the best investigators in our department and a horse's ass, was also a dirty cop.

A gust of wind from the north sent a chill through me. "What do you want me to do?" I asked quietly.

"I called Pete in. I'm going to give him the lead. He works well with Sam in internal. Sam's going to be handling the use-of-force report on Nichols."

"And since Pete and I work as partners most of the time..."

"It will seem natural that you're close to the case. Of course, Matt will still have to be involved a bit since he took the lead in the second rape."

"What a mess," I said, shaking my head.

Another car pulled up next to the crime scene van and Pete Henley's large bulk emerged. He looked around for a minute before he spotted us and came over. In his mid-forties and a little over three hundred pounds, with a wife and two teenage daughters that were the center of his world, Pete's easygoing nature fooled a lot of people. But he was a natural investigator and the best shot in the department.

In Adams County, Pete was the man with his ear to the ground. He knew everybody in our small, rural north Florida county. For most families, he could tell you their history going back for as many generations as they'd lived here. He was also well tuned into local politics, so he didn't need to have the pitfalls of the current situation spelled out for him.

Dad told Pete he was the lead investigator and filled him in on what little information he had.

"I'm on it," Pete said with reluctance. He turned and walked over to the crime scene tape, lifting it up, and awkwardly slipped under it.

"Go on," Dad said to me, looking over at the news crews who were done shooting background footage of the scene and were heading toward us. I avoided making eye contact with the reporters as I hurried under the tape.

The bodies were located at the back of a small shopping center. The woman's body was half hidden behind a dumpster near a loading dock. Five feet away was the man's body, curled up and face down on the pavement. I never would have recognized him as Ayers. Marcus and Shantel were methodically taking pictures from different angles.

"Do we know her name?" Pete asked Deputy Julio Ortiz, who was standing well back from the bodies.

"She is... was Angie Maitland. I went to school with her."

Julio was about five years younger than me, twenty-five maybe. Around the sheriff's office he was always hanging out with the clowns, the guys that razzed each other, came up with silly practical jokes and challenged each other to weightlifting or running contests. There were no jokes tonight, though, his voice sad and dismayed. In a small county like ours, you realized pretty early that the car wreck you responded to or the domestic disturbance call you answered might involve someone you knew. It made a hard job harder. And was one of the reasons I'd rather have been doing something else.

"Has her family been informed?" Pete asked.

"I don't know."

Pete pulled out his radio and checked with dispatch. No one had contacted the family. "Would you to do it?" Pete asked Julio.

"Sure," Julio nodded, turning away to get the address from dispatch.

"What about Ayers?" I asked Pete.

"We'd better do it. We'll go over after we talk with Nichols."

Pete watched Marcus and Shantel work for another couple of minutes. "Hold up, guys," he said when they both lowered their cameras for a moment.

Pete turned and shouted to the other deputies standing around, "Turn off all the headlights for a couple minutes!" It took a second for everyone to process what he'd said, but slowly two of them went to the cars and turned off the lights.

"Take some pictures," he told the vague shadows of Marcus and Shantel.

It was very dark behind the store with the headlights off. Streetlights glowed in the distance, but that just seemed to amplify the darkness near the loading dock.

After a minute Pete shouted, "Nichols, turn on your lights!" The headlights of a car parked fifty feet away came on, illuminating the bodies while casting stark shadows against the back wall of the building. Pete asked Marcus and Shantel for a few more pictures, then finally shouted for everyone to turn the lights back on.

"Let's go talk with Nichols," he said to me.

I followed him over to where Deputy Isaac Nichols leaned against his patrol car. First thing I noticed was that his holster was empty.

"They already bagged it," he said when he saw us looking

at his holster.

"Don't think you have much to worry about," Pete responded.

"I know it's standard procedure, just like the suspension. Still hard to take," Nichols said mournfully. "I just wished I'd gotten here in time to save her. I damn sure don't regret shooting him."

Pete held up his hand. "Careful what you say. Breathe deep." I could see Nichols was still shaking from the adrenaline dump his system had received.

"You don't have to tell me. I'm not going to give my formal statement for a couple days."

This was the advice we all received during our training. Memory is notoriously unreliable right after a traumatic event, and actually becomes more accurate a couple days later. If you make a detailed statement right after a shooting, you're probably going to regret it. There will be details that don't fit and that you know to be wrong, but if you change your story then the damage is done and you risk being grilled by attorneys on both sides of the aisle during a trial.

"I don't want details right now. Just give me the rough outline of what went down," Pete requested.

"When I drove back here, I heard a scream and I saw the guy on top of the woman. I didn't know who he was. I got out and told him to get up. He didn't. I ran over toward them and all of a sudden he turned and came at me. I saw a knife in his hand. Pulled my gun and fired twice." There was a tremor in Nichols's voice. His hands twisted and kneaded each other. "I never thought I'd be the guy that had to shoot someone."

"Why'd you drive back here?" Pete asked the question that had been upper-most in my mind.

"My field training officer showed me this spot. I've caught prostitutes, people doing drugs... Once I caught some guy that was dumping a couple purses he'd stolen." All of that could be checked easily.

Pete patted him on the back. "We'll get this cleared up.

HR will set you up with someone to talk to."

"I don't know," Nichols said, answering some question that only he heard. "It's been a crazy night."

Pete and I walked away, not talking until we were out of his hearing. "They found a knife?" Pete asked me.

"I got here just a few minutes before you did. I didn't see one, but maybe it's under the body. Let's go find out."

As we walked back toward the bodies, I saw Dad standing under a floodlight as he was interviewed by one of the news crews from Tallahassee. His voice was loud and deep. "I take full responsibility for any decision made by my office."

Dad could irritate the crap out of me, but I'd never doubted his integrity or dedication to his job. After my mother died, Dad was lost without her, so I'd encouraged him to run for sheriff as a way to redirect his attention. He'd been a deputy for half his life and I knew there was no one in the county who could do a better job. Being sheriff saved him and did a lot to improve the lives of the people of Adams County.

I noticed the coroner's van had been added to the growing number of random vehicles arranged like vultures flocking to fresh roadkill. Marcus and Shantel were standing back, filming the body of Jeffrey Ayers as Dr. Darzi examined it. I was surprised to see him. Normally, his participation was limited to the actual autopsy. Dad must have called him personally. With an officer's career and Dad's reelection in the balance, it was vital that the investigation be above reproach.

Ayers's body was probed, measured and handled with detached professionalism, leaving no doubt that he was now more a piece of evidence than a person.

"Little help," Dr. Darzi said to no one in particular. Marcus went over and gave him a hand turning the body onto its side. Sure enough, there was a six-inch-long folding knife, blade out, lying underneath. Darzi examined the corpse's back. "Looks like one of the bullets went through him. The other probably broke up or is lodged against a bone or in an organ." We would have to look for the bullet that went through the body.

Shantel and Marcus moved in and emptied Ayers's pockets, bagging and tagging everything. Finally the body was lifted onto a gurney and moved to the coroner's van. Darzi then went over and began the same process with the woman's body.

"At least they found a knife," Pete said to me in a low voice. He hated the press and they were still hovering around, though they had enough respect for the victims to stay back and keep their cameras off the scene. The South had changed a lot, for both good and ill, but most of us still had some respect for the dead. It was a mix of superstition and awe brought on by being in the presence of the ultimate mystery.

"But did Ayers kill the woman?" I asked Pete.

"Not with a knife," Dr. Darzi answered. "There are no cuts on the body. She appears, only appears, mind you, to have been strangled." He probed around her neck and revealed a rope that had been pulled so tight that it was hidden under the flesh of her throat.

"I can't decide whether this is good or bad," Pete said. "Looks good for Nichols and bad for the sheriff." Pete looked around. "Where is Ayers's car?"

We went on a hunt for it and found it parked in front of the store. "That's odd. It's not parked in a space," I said.

"Not like anyone's going to complain." Pete indicated the empty lot. "Pretty strange he'd park out here and drag her around back."

"Maybe he saw her walking toward the back and followed her."

We both shrugged. This early in the investigation, there were just too many questions.

We walked back to the scene and Pete told Shantel where the car was and that they'd need to process it tonight. It would be towed back to our small impound lot, a quarter acre of asphalt behind the sheriff's office with a ten-foot fence topped by concertina wire.

"Okay now, if you're going to start telling us how to do everything, you may as well have the B Team out here. You know you got the A Team, so let us do our thing." Shantel was always ready to throw around the banter. That and the fact she and Marcus were the best forensics team in north Florida were the main reasons we all liked working with them.

"I'd never think of telling you how to do your business," Pete said with a smile.

"You better not, big man, or you can get down here and crawl around on your hands and knees looking for God knows what," Shantel said as she moved around the bodies with her headlamp focused six inches in front of her, looking for anything that might turn out to be important trace evidence.

I turned to Pete. "We know how Ayers got here. It would help to know Angie Maitland's movements."

"Let's go tell Ayers's family what's happened. We've got time to figure out why Maitland was here," Pete said, and we headed for his car.

This was a different dynamic for us. Normally we'd split up and handle different tasks, then come back together and compare notes. But I think neither of us wanted to take the risk of missing something in a case this complicated. With ten months to go until the election, Dad's main opponent, Charles Maxwell, Calhoun's chief of police, was already campaigning heavily. He and Dad had never gotten along and Chief Maxwell was sure to use this case as ammunition.

No one likes to do notifications. There are a dozen different ways they can play out and few of them are good. I've known deputies that were attacked by family members and others that couldn't leave because they were afraid a friend or relative might hurt themselves.

Jeffrey Ayers had been in his mid-thirties, but still lived at home with his mother. Not that surprising these days. Hers was a one-story ranch-style house in a middle-class neighborhood north of Calhoun. All the windows were dark when we pulled into the driveway. Looking at my watch, it was almost one-thirty. I closed my door carefully when I got out of the car, so as not to disturb everyone in the neighborhood. But as soon as the door clicked shut, one dog after another started barking. What can you do?

Pete walked heavily up to the door and rang the bell. It took two more tries before the porch light came on and a voice from inside asked who we were. We produced names and badges, then the door was opened by a surprisingly young-looking woman. She didn't look a day over fifty, even after being woken in the middle of the night.

"What's happened?" she asked, holding the door open for us to come in. She was wearing a blue robe and kept smoothing her hair as though she wished that she could brush it. "Is Jeffrey all right?"

"I'm sorry," Pete said quietly.

"Oh, my God. What?" She looked like she was going to collapse, so I put my hand on her arm and eased her down onto a wingback chair.

"Mrs. Ayers, I'm sorry, but your son is dead," I said, not wanting to drag it out. She knew something horrible had happened so what good would it do to delay the inevitable?

"How?" she asked.

I didn't want to tell her, but I didn't seem to be able to stop myself. "One of our deputies shot him."

"What? Why? Why did you kill my son?" She was pounding her fists on the arms of the chair so hard that it rocked back and forth. I knew that she really wanted to be hitting us.

Pete seemed at a loss. "Our deputy reported that your son was assaulting a woman and, when he ordered him to stop, your son turned and charged. The deputy had to defend himself."

"Lies!" she screamed. "All of those lies you told about him. He never hurt anyone!" She stopped pounding the chair and brought her hands up in front of her.

I knew what was going to happen a nanosecond before she flew out of the chair and started flailing at me.

I just curled up and let her thump me with her fists. Pete tried to get in between us and deflect some of the blows.

"Please stop now," Pete said. "I'm investigating the shooting. If your son's death wasn't justified, I promise we'll set the record straight."

Mrs. Ayers landed a few more blows, but her strength was fading. Finally she dropped back into the chair and began to sob.

"Is there someone you could call?" I asked gently.

"I have to tell Wayne," she said and then began crying again. I vaguely remembered that Jeffrey Ayers had a brother.

"Is that your other son?"

"Yes," she said, trying to control her sobbing. "He didn't do it. Jeffrey, he was here the night that girl was attacked. I know that."

During an interview regarding one of the rapes, she had told us that she'd heard Ayers come home and hadn't heard him go out again. But she had also admitted it was possible she could have fallen asleep and not heard him go back out.

"Where is he?" she asked. Tears still rolled down her face, but her breathing was coming under control.

"We have to take his body to the… hospital for an autopsy. We want the truth as much as you do," Pete told her.

"I can't think. Go. I don't want you all here."

"Do you want us to call your son?" I asked.

"No, just get out. I'll call him. Go. You've done enough!" she shouted. We quietly made our escape.

ACKNOWLEDGMENTS

Many thanks to my beta readers—Chuck Mitchell, Jan Lydon and especially Locke Haney, who discovered a small, yet significant, problem with the plot.

I never would have had the courage to attempt self-publishing without the constant support and encouragement of H. Y. Hanna. She has provided an endless supply of valuable lists, resources and advice. She was invaluable as a beta reader and developed a great cover design for the series. Words cannot express my appreciation for all her help.

Good fortune smiled on me when I met a woman who could be my friend, my editor and my wife. Many things in my life, including this series, could not be accomplished without Melanie by my side.

Original Cover Design by H. Y. Hanna
Paperback Cover Design by Robin Ludwig Design Inc.
www.gobookcoverdesign.com

ABOUT THE AUTHOR

A. E. Howe lives and writes on a farm in the wilds of north Florida with his wife, horses and more cats than he can count. He received a degree in English Education from the University of Georgia and is a produced screenwriter and playwright. His first published book was *Broken State*; the Larry Macklin Mysteries is his first series and he has plans for more. Howe is also the co-host of the "Guns of Hollywood" podcast, part of the Firearms Radio Network. When not writing or podcasting, Howe enjoys riding, competitive shooting and working on the farm.